# THE DANCER
# WITH A DODGY KNEE

# THE DANCER

## WITH A DODGY KNEE

Larry Signy

Flamenco dancer image made by Freepik from www.flaticon.com

First paperback edition

978-1-80541-372-1 (paperback)
978-1-80541-374-5 (hardcover)
978-1-80541-373-8 (eBook)

# Contents

# Chapter 1

# DANCE, BALLERINA, DANCE

The music was a slow, balletic song, and the girl's movements matched it perfectly.

Pirouettes, arabesques and jumps. All delicate movements in a mature, well-trained way, a poetic combination of fast and slow turns that defied her age.

Light-coloured sequins on her bodice reflected the floodlights set way behind the audience, and more lights from the wings picked out the silver spangles on her small tutu. It not only looked good; it was technically good as well, far better than the grubby old stage deserved.

Although she was only young, it was all there, a whirling, enchanting performance that, from the start, won the audience's combined hearts and was shown by the ovation at the end. Some people in the middle of the stalls stood to applaud.

On stage, Charlene Whittaker curtseyed, smiling. She faced left, right, centre, and bobbed down. The audience wouldn't stop.

After a moment or two, someone backstage started the next piece of music—something lively in contrast to the sweet tenderness of the main dance. It was meant to cover the dancer's exit from the stage but instead, Charlene got caught up in the music again and began a small shimmy, then—still wearing her pink ballet shoes—swept effortlessly into a rigorous soundless tap. The audience whooped and whistled, thinking it was still part of the show.

"Come off," cried the stage manager in a semi-stage whisper.

The dancer took no notice.

"If you don't come off *now*, I'm coming on to drag you off," said a more uncompromising, authoritarian voice.

Reluctantly, and with the audience still applauding, the dancer took a giant balletic leap into the wings.

"How unprofessional," said her father, the second unbending voice. "You've been to plenty of these shows. You should know how to make an exit by now."

The girl smiled back. She was still dancing in her mind, celebrating her birthday. This was the day she became six.

# AUDITIONS

The memory came back to Charlene—now approaching twenty and known to everyone as Charlie—as she turned up for what promised to be a big audition day for her. It was not her own usual, casual call; this time she had been specially invited to test for a part in a big West End musical show to be called *That Girl Next Door*, and Charlie had been told that "early recognition" by several of the producer's talent staff had led to her being picked out for a possible leading to a role in it.

She later found the "talent staff" consisted of his family and friends who had been called on to help, mostly financially, during his first show and who had happened to see her in the provinces. Despite his previous successes, the producer, Aaron Blomfield, did not have any real staff except for one secretary, his wife.

Charlie had been to many, many auditions, most of them organised by her father when she was very young, and since becoming a professional had, like most unknown hopefuls, attended more simply hoping to be chosen for a role, no matter how small. Mostly, they had been fruitless, although she once won a secondary non-singing role in a West End production that ran for just three weeks, and she had won a small part in an out-of-town provincial show after taking part in another audition.

But she had been called in specially for this one and was surprised when she then found herself treated as at every other trial she had attended: being asked to stand on one side waiting for the producer to turn up to run his eye over her and coldly dissect her looks and talents. She had anticipated that, as she had been specifically invited, she was there to read and sing for a specific part.

But still, now she was there amongst all the other would-be hoofers testing for a role in a West End show and she was excited although it was so different from what she expected. She arrived a little before the set time to find a roomful of other young hopefuls—no boys, just girls—and while they all waited, the rehearsal pianist played some of the music from the new show. Charlie enjoyed listening to the songs, her foot tapping and her body mentally swaying to some of the intricate rhythms. When producer Aaron arrived accompanied by the show's two young song writers—Harry McIntyre and lyricist Danny Grover, the men behind the huge hits *The Age of Romance* and *Doctors and Nurses*—she saw a copy of some of the lyrics for the first time as well.

"What d'you think of them?" asked Danny, who had come over to stand by her.

Charlie nodded, approving.

"No need to tell us how good they are. That's my job. I wrote them," joked Danny.

Charlie blushed. "But... but they are good..." It sounded lame.

Danny laughed. "Don't worry," he said as he walked off. "I'm sure you'll be hearing a lot more of 'em."

Aaron and Danny's partner Harry McIntyre had sat down behind a long desk by the side of the pianist, and Danny returned to them. He sat on a corner of the desk, one foot on the floor and the other dangling, and the three men chatted quietly and earnestly as the piano played on. Charlie looked at them closely, wondering what they were like. Her future depended on it.

Aaron was surprisingly short and slight, a dapper man, slim, balding with grey hair and a heavy brown moustache, wearing an expensively smart suit and tie. Although he always seemed a bit of an idiot and a charlatan, he was hard-working for his shows, casts and crews and always did all he could to help them.

Beside him, Harry also wore a suit and tie. He was good-looking, seemingly quiet and introverted, and Charlie had already guessed that the tall, gangling, humorous-looking Danny—casually, almost untidily dressed in sweater and jeans—was the live wire of the three.

Danny said something, and the other two looked over at Charlie, and the girl felt herself blushing again.

The songs for the new show were good, the lyrics tremendous and right for the music. Charlie knew they were the perfect combination for a musical, and she loved them and hoped she would get a chance to sing and dance them.

As the audition began, it became quite obvious that Aaron had wanted the stars of his first two shows—Toni Benito and Julia Ross—to continue their partnership, but Julia was not available and Toni was recording an album, and the writers wanted a new pairing in any case.

Like all the other girls, Charlie had handed in her CV and a head-shot photo as soon as she arrived at the audition. Now she waited.

The three men, producer and writers, sat behind the long, bare, wooden table and began the slow process of weeding through the assembled audition hopefuls ranged around the rehearsal room, being quite ruthless in some cases, one or other of them nodding slight approval occasionally, rarely smiling, but always alert and attentive to what was going on. Some of the candidates were good, some bad. Some could sing but not dance. Some could dance but not sing. But the judging trio listened to them all politely, without a word.

Charlie watched with dispassionate detachment. It was not up to her to judge, but she couldn't help from keeping an eye on what was now the "opposition".

Then she was jerked back to reality. Her name was called. It was her turn.

She stepped forwards a little self-consciously, handed a music sheet to the pianist, heard Aaron say he wanted her to sing first then dance to the same song, then took a deep, slow breath to try to calm herself. When the audition pianist began playing, she heard the first notes, and for a few bars she was almost on automatic pilot. Then her nerves settled, and she got into the mood of the song.

It was a tune from the writers' first show and she knew it well. After ending the lyrics, she began to move—switching effortlessly from voice to dance. Suddenly, the music took over, although the lyrics kept going through her mind automatically to help her keep to the rhythm.

Suddenly, the tempo changed. Danny had asked the pianist to speed it up so he could see if the dancer could cope with a switch. Charlie let herself go, and swung, tapped and floated her way to the end. It was almost like her dance on her sixth birthday.

When it was over, the pianist nodded approval, and as Charlie went back to a place by a far wall, she heard the producer and writers chatting about the various applicants. She heard Danny, the lyricist, talking about the girls.

"Why do some of them bother with skirts? It's getting so it's hard to tell which is higher, the waistline or the hemline."

She thought he hadn't taken any notice of her singing his words or dancing, that he couldn't like girls, that she had no chance with him. But then he began raving about one of the contestants—she didn't hear a name—her looks, her voice and her dance skills, and suggested she would be ideal for the part.

After about five minutes, Charlie heard her name called out and saw Aaron nodding in her direction. She took two or three hesitant steps forwards towards the table again. She felt that everything in the audition hall had stopped. Suddenly, there was no piano, and she knew all the other dancers had their eyes on her, envious. She semi-stopped, taking a half step, but then Danny smiled and beckoned her forwards.

Behind her, she heard an assistant, apparently miles away, thanking the other girls and telling them the audition was over.

She knew it was a cliche, but she was almost in a dream as Aaron offered her the lead role in the new show.

"I wanted you all along—ever since I saw you in that show, twice—and I paid for the tickets both times," said Aaron genially. "But I called you to a general audition because I wanted the boys to pick you out for themselves. They both agree with me. You're the girl..."

What he didn't tell her was that from the start of her audition, the two song writers had both told him they thought she had that indefinable something that had nothing to do with her undoubted talent and ability—something that was star quality.

Charlie did a little jig, giggled, blushed and then didn't know what to do with herself.

"Come to the office tomorrow and we'll sort out a contract," said Aaron.

Danny stepped round the table to put an arm round her shoulder. "Bring an agent if you've got one," he said. "Aaron's a shark..."

When Charlie went to Aaron's office the next day, it was to discuss the show and her role, and she casually explained that she didn't have an agent. She naively said she wasn't worried so much about the money but just wanted a chance. Aaron mentally noted the money angle, then smoothly said he would work on her behalf if she was willing. Not surprisingly, he did not mention his percentage cut of her earnings, but said he would prepare a contract.

He made a note on a pad on his desk. *Find a copy of an agent's contract form from somewhere,* he wrote, and called in his secretary and handed it to her.

Charlie had no thoughts of agents or interest payments, but she was simply delighted that she had been offered the joint lead with a young male singer and dancer, Adam Knowles, who was beginning to become a bit of a "name". Her contract was for the run of the show, and it offered Charlie more money than she had ever earned before. She was delighted with it, and happily signed the contract witnessed by Aaron's secretary, the producer's harsh-faced, harsh-sounding wife.

# GROWING UP

aiting for rehearsals to begin only took three weeks, but for Charlie it seemed an eternity. And although she tried not to think about it, her mind couldn't help remembering the path that had led her to the point of starring in a West End show. As she waited, she remembered her childhood.

She had always loved to dance, and it now seemed to her that she had always been destined for the position she now found herself in. Although her mother had wanted to call her Andrea, her father had insisted that Charlene Whittaker would look better outside a theatre "when she became a famous dancer". She had been given both names when her mother said either would look good on the posters.

Luckily, Charlene Andrea had grown up finding music and rhythm in everything, and instead of skipping along would often be seen at her mother's side twirling round and round as they walked amongst the streets. People would be amused even when she bumped into them and bowed before dancing off again.

She had always loved dancing, and her delight in performing to music was obvious from her earliest days. Her mother encouraged her to join classes almost as soon as she could walk, and after just a couple of years she performed at many local fetes and village shows, becoming something of a celebrity with her natural instinct for dancing and cute way of holding her audience. She was what can only be described as a mop-haired, curly blonde in the style of Shirley Temple, although she always imagined herself to be more like Dorothy in *The Wizard of Oz*.

Because of her regular performances, she grew up in a mini world of auditions, because for some reason local show directors always imagined themselves as big West End or Broadway impresarios and insisted on running casting trials even though they knew practically everyone who applied to take part. Although it was all strictly amateur, they pretended to anyone who would listen that they were putting on "their show" in a professional manner. But the amateurness showed.

Charlie loved the dancing and the show routines. But she was also glad of the periods between them when she could spend time with her mother. They would often go out on sunny days for what her mother called "fun girlie days"—the most popular place was Newlands Corner near Guildford, and she would never forget her mother looking over the view there and talking about Lorenz Hart's "Mountain Greenery".

"Truly," she would say, "A place where God paints the scenery."

Charlie loved the place herself so much that she would invariably start to dance on the grass down the hill in sheer joy at its beauty, but she also kept in mind that one day she lost her footing on the grass and went rolling down the slope hooting with laughter, with her mother's echoing laughter as she watched. Later, when they got home and she excitedly told her father about it, he had told her off, and sternly warned her that she might hurt her ankles badly, which would stop her dancing. She remembered that.

Another day, they were driving through the back byways near their home and her mother said she loved the roads in the country.

"I love the way the trees grow over the top so it's like driving through a natural avenue," she said. And she laughed. "It really is 'a Surrey with a fringe o'er the top'."

Charlie had not been certain she understood, but she also liked the trees and didn't say anything.

Often, they would stop outside a small, lonely country house with gabled windows and two enormously tall chimneys.

"It's a storybook cottage," said Charlie's mother. And she would tell of the people who had once lived there. "This old squire got married and brought his young bride there..."

She would start in a messianic, irreverent voice and would tell the young girl a tale, a grisly tale, of fantasy woven around the house that, despite its horrific gory nature, would have them both shrieking out loud with laughter.

Then there was the old lady they often saw walking her horse with her pet dog perched on the saddle in front of her, and she and her mother would exchange smiles and get a glowing smile in return. Then her mother would weave a story of lost romance in which the woman's husband had been turned into her pet by a wicked lord of the manor!

Charlie loved the stories, and also the times she and her mother would energetically climb through the sun-dappled woods behind their house to the top of a steep hill where, in her memory and twilight dreaming, she would see again the misty merging of one layer of hills into the next, always with a thin wisp of smoke from a chimney down in one of the valleys. She would always remember through the mists of her mind the beauty of it all —the green fields falling beyond the trees below them with an occasional splodge of yellow.

Once, while they were sitting at the top of the hill looking over the view, a robin landed and perched on the ground in front of them, puffing out his red breast and cocking his head on one side, stamping his feet around in the dust. He looked at them both quizzically.

"Isn't he lovely? And he's dancing for us," cried Charlie.

"He's only letting us know that this is his place, just trying to show that he's the boss around here," said her mother. "But yes, I think he really wants to let us know that we're almost his equals."

Always though, there were the never-ending auditions.

Although she disliked being called to try-outs, where she was usually talked over and about but never to, the young Charlie quickly became used to the life, putting up with it all because of her love for dancing. Her biggest performance was when she was seven, and her father took her to play Brigitta in *The Sound of Music*, a performance that ran no less than fourteen times, including matinees, at a leisure centre near Milton Keynes.

*Sound* was to lead to many, many similar shows as Charlie grew. With them, her dancing improved, and soon she grew too good for her school and she was switched to a new one where she was likely to get a more varied dance education.

She loved to dance, but she didn't like her new teacher and the continual snobbish use of the recognised and approved ballet terms that she threw out. Adagio, allegro, arabesque, petit jeté, plié and chaseé. Glissade, en pointe, passé, pirouette, grand fouette. Charlie quite liked the flic-flac, a movement touching the toe to the side, then to the front, then putting it near the ankle of the other leg, but only because she liked the sound of it, and while she had the differences between the brisé dessus and the brisé dessous drummed into her young mind, she really couldn't care less about either of them. She didn't want to talk about all the moves using their names—she just wanted to get on and perform them.

And perform them she did, at the many continuing small town and village amateur shows. She thoroughly enjoyed the excitement and glamour of these shows, even the smallest, but by the time she was eleven, she had begun to dread the weekly formalities of the ballet classes she had to attend.

Charlie would often break out from the unbending lessons to put in steps and movements that infuriated her teacher so much that at the end of term, she sent a complaint to her parents. Banished from the ballet school, Charlie went instead to a more relaxed male teacher who liked all kinds of dance and encouraged her to form her own way of doing things.

Charlie carried on dancing, and things improved quite quickly. She loved the new style she began to develop as the new teacher helped her with a more modern style. She loved the music of stage musicals, and found it helped her find her own rhythms and movements.

Five weeks after she started in the new school though, Charlie's mother died. Neither Charlie nor her father grieved publicly, nor, indeed, together. They both endured the loss in their own minds.

Charlie carried on dancing, improving almost lesson by lesson with her new teacher, and slowly their lives returned to normal. As she got better, her father pushed her even harder, even when her feet were bleeding, he made her practise until she was as near perfect as she could be.

Surprisingly, he liked the new style Charlie was developing, and told her about her mother's ambitions as a young girl.

"Your mother always wanted to be a dancer," he told her. "When we got married, she desperately wanted to be in a West End show, but she had to make a home. Then you came along and she had no chance."

Because of his insistence, Charlie would spend hours every day practising her formal dance routines. Only rarely did she get time off, although a few weeks after her mother's death, she did manage to persuade her father to take her for a country drive along the roads her mother had driven her and which she knew so well. As they went, she pointed to the birds on the telephone wires, their tails wagging as they danced in the sunshine.

"They're just keeping their feet warm," he replied briskly, and soon they were home. It was not the same.

He had always said that she should learn to dance while she was young and still small—he had heard that a dancer should start training before growing up so her muscles would grow the right way—and Charlie had always accepted it without complaint. Dance was life for her—everything she had ever wanted—although other parts of her life, friends, education, having fun, all went by the board. When she turned eleven, Charlie and her father were well known on "the circuit".

They often went to the expensive "name" restaurants locally, ostensibly as a treat but always so Charlie's father could show her off in front of the amateur producers he invariably knew would be there, some whom he invited along. Occasional professional agents were happy to get a free meal—Charlie's father just wanted his girl to be seen, although most times he ignored her throughout the meal and she sat in a lonely state often giggling with the waiters or waitresses when her father did not notice. Quite often, she would order the meal she wanted only for her father to tell the waiter what she really "wanted" was something else.

It was a role reversal. It was Charlie's father who was just like the traditional "real professional mum". He wanted to atone for the success he had deprived his wife of through his daughter, and he pressed and pushed uncompromisingly to get it. It was, he justified, what her mother had really wanted.

Charlie really loved the performing, even when her father and often her teacher railed against her for drifting off into her own magical world of make-believe, weaving steps that bore no relation to what she had been taught and dancing by juvenile instinct rather than in the way she was told she should. She just loved to dance, she would forsake her dolls and other toys to perform to audiences—unseen except in her own eyes and imagination—in her bedroom or living room. She would hear the music, dance the steps, and take untold bows and curtsies to rapturous applause. As the "woman of the house", she took care of a lot of the mundane tasks, and one day, when her father was out, she was dusting around with the radio on, listening to *Desert Island Discs.* She listened as she worked, and then, from the radio, came the famous old version of "Cheek to Cheek" sung by Fred *Astaire*

in his lovely melodic dancer's voice, and after listening for a moment, Charlie found herself swaying along with it. "Imagine," she said, "Me, dancing with Fred Astaire." Charlie became a huge replacement of a wife for her father, and over the next few years, he pushed her towards the stage so her childhood became a long, almost suffocating round of auditions, dance lessons, school, and occasionally some small parts in small-time shows.

She had started as a six-year-old child prodigy—her father pushing her and forcing her to go to auditions and be cute. She loved the dancing and the music, but at the time she hated the "stage dad" actions that pushed her into "war" with the other kids as he tried to force producers into making her a star.

By the time Charlie reached her mid-teens, however, her father began to tire of his role as pusher-of-talent. He became half-hearted about her ambitions, and he let Charlie get on with things on her own. As she grew up, she began working on her own and at her own pace, continuing to dance and still going to as many auditions as she could in an effort to make the break and become a professional dancer.

Local producers and agents quickly got to know her home telephone number, and at first, she was thrilled when the phone rang. But after a few months, she began to dread the shrill reverberations and the repeated answering mantra, "793058". It more often than not heralded yet another call to yet another of the dreaded auditions she had started to hate so much. But although she didn't like the process, it was different to before—no one was making her go to the trials and they were something she had to endure if she wanted to make it as a "real" dancer.

Charlie yearned for a "normal" teenage life, but was always restricted by her father's tired exhortations to go to bed early, to sleep, to train, to perform. She would often dream of creeping out in the night and wandering the streets to the city centre for an hour or two just watching, enjoying, life happening all around her. In her dream, she would stand in the shadows outside pubs and clubs looking at the youngsters there seemingly enjoying themselves, and she had moments when she wished she could join them and dance with them. But she knew it wouldn't be the same kind of dancing she enjoyed.

One day, she did actually stay awake until her father had gone to bed and after a while, crept out of her bedroom, making her way downstairs being careful to only use the edges of the stair treads because she had read that was what burglars did to stop them creaking. She intended on following her dream, but when it came to it, she was too scared to leave the house, and quickly crept back to her bedroom where she fell into a deep sleep almost immediately.

Mostly though, Charlie's life consisted of training and occasionally performing. Even between times at home she would work on her warm-up routines, while at lessons there was all the stretching, the barre work, tap practice and the rest. She wanted to learn how to sing properly, rather than to just warble the notes, and she took voice lessons and breathing exercises. It was all to get her stamina up, to get physically and mentally fit for what could be a long run.

Her father was pushing her less now, but for a while, he was around when she went to the shows she had arranged. But he was noticeably slowing down, and soon even stopped that, rarely even asking her how she had got on.

The day he died was a peculiar day for Charlie. She felt sad. After all, he was the one who had pushed her until she got a start as a dancer, but she felt devoid of emotion. She insisted on going on stage in a local hall that evening "as a tribute to Daddy", and it wasn't until the day of the funeral that his death really hit her.

At the crematorium, she looked at the coffin, and as it slid away at the end of the service, she had a sudden feeling of loss. While she didn't feel as if she had killed him—as so many do—she felt in some way responsible for the fact that she would never see him again. But now, she had no parents—she was on her own.

# Chapter 4

# SHOW BIZ

**A**fter her father's death, Charlie rented out their house in the country and moved into a temporary flat in a London suburb while she looked for somewhere closer to the West End and the heart of London show land.

By now, Charlie's dance style had developed. As a youngster, her lessons had been largely aimed at making her like all ballet dancers—trained to move their bodies in unnatural ways and make it look natural. But now she had developed a style that was a mix of ballet, ballroom, tap and other bits that she incorporated as her own. And she could sing—in fact, her voice was quite lyrical when used for more popular show songs rather than great arias.

On her own, she took part in as many trials and workshop calls as possible, and after a couple of small one-night-only shows she eventually got a part with a local rep at a fairly large theatre twenty miles out of London as one of the featured singer–dancers in a tour of a moderate West End hit. She took over a medium-sized role from another dancer who had been pulled into the company's newest pre-London show.

Charlie had now changed her hair from her baby tight blonde curls into a light auburn in colour and fashioned it into a sleek layered cut, fringing her forehead and falling to her shoulders in a way that meant she could tie it back when she danced. She was very slightly above average height, and she had an exquisite, classic British-beauty face—not conventional prettiness but striking. Her cheekbones were high, her eyes an arresting blue looking out from what used to be called a peaches-and-cream complexion, and she didn't need to wear make-up to make people look at her in the street. She had grown into a beautiful woman.

She still loved to dance. And dance. She liked the rehearsals as well as the shows themselves, and she enjoyed the thrill of dancing professionally and working with other professional dancers. She had no jealousy for any of them, but watched and took on board any of the good ideas they seemed to show.

It was a busy life. The show was booked for a rare six-week run "in the sticks", and Charlie quickly got into a routine where she looked after her temporary flat and did shopping and things like that in the mornings, went to rehearsals in the afternoons unless there was a matinee—every Tuesday and Saturday—and then went to the evening performance. Busy, busy. But Charlie loved every moment.

She made friends with the other girls in the cast, and enjoyed late night after-show suppers with them in their flats. Hers was too small to invite friends in, so they often went to small coffee bars or cafes, where the talk was still invariably about getting to the West End: the "Big Time".

"When I'm a name, I'm going to set up a fund for wannabe actresses like us," one would insist.

"Oh no, you'll be too busy for that," replied another.

"Well, I'll just get... er... my people to fix it!"

Charlie enjoyed being part of the company and was accepted. She did not have any grand ideas. Just that she wanted to get a part—any part—in a West End musical show. Somewhere she could dance for an audience.

There were some niggles, of course. One day, one of the girls was sick and a rumour quickly went round that she was pregnant.

"Oh, *hors de combat*," one of the male dancers said, emphasising the first h. "She hurt her back while working!"

Charlie was just one of several of the other girls to stick up for the ailing girl.

At the same time, most Sundays when she was not working or taking classes, she enjoyed going "home" to pick up her normal mid-Surrey life. The family house was now occupied by an ageing aunt, the sister of her father, who lived alone, but although she kept the house as immaculate as it had been when Charlie was a girl, things had been moved, collections scattered—it was altered. Charlie had grown up with the chintz three-piece suite in the living room alongside a cabinet with the best "posh" cups, saucers, teapots and milk jugs— with all the handles lined up by her father and pointing in the same direction like a military formation. The whole feel was now different.

Yet, despite her growing maturity and her working show business environment, she still found extreme happiness amongst her friendly and homely childhood surroundings.

Charlie provided temporary companionship for the aunt, who was a nice old girl but frail. She enjoyed it more when she went out for walks alone and saw that the house round the corner with the terribly trim, three-tiered garden was still as well-cared for as when she used to see it while out with her mother, and the old Elizabethan "Christmas card" mansion at the bottom of the hill was still as imposing.

Sometimes, when she passed them, she would talk to her mother.

"Mummy, do you think they have a magnificent ballroom with a tall ceiling, where the owners and their guests can dance the night away in long, flowing ball gowns—with servants bringing them everything they could possibly want to make the night complete?"

In her mind, she could hear her mother's tinkling laugh at the thought.

She still loved to climb the wooded hills behind the house, gazing up at the tall trees, wondering as she had as a child how a tiny pine needle could turn into something so magnificent and big. In her mind, she would hear her mother laughing while she, as a five-year-old, would turn serious and say the many dead branches that had sprouted as the trees grew stuck out like the arms of a ballet dancer.

By now she had a regular boyfriend, David Walsh, and he would often come to rehearsals to watch her, although he would off-handedly tell her that she would have to give up working when they were married. One weekend, Charlie took him home to show him where she had grown up. He and her aunt did not get on, and David made several rather unpleasant remarks about the rich people of Surrey.

"Real socialist territory," he sneered.

"We're not rich at all. In fact, as my husband used to say, you could say we're only just the nouveau middle class," replied her aunt tartly.

The weekend was not a success.

But there were still her show friends. Charlie had a special pal in the show, Bo Daniels—her real name was Margaret, but everyone called her Bo after the song "Mr Bojangles"—who shared a dressing room with her. They got along well, had the same background, the same sense of fun. And both loved to dance. They shared secrets.

Slowly, despite her visits home, Charlie's life was changing and show business—and dancing—were more the focus of her whole being. But that last weekend still had an effect. About four or five weeks after it, Charlie got a phone call from David ending their romance. That day, following afternoon rehearsals, the pianist carried on tinkling away, and Charlie started to dance to the classic song "Dance, Ballerina, Dance".

The line in the song about dancers *having* to dance came to her mind as she whirled and tapped in rhythm thinking of David's face. Charlie pirouetted and turned, suddenly noticing the empty seat where he usual sat, while the pianist carried on, seemingly ignoring her.

Charlie concentrated on the music, but there was a different feel to her dancing. It was more intense, more personal. She had subconsciously learnt how to add emotion to her natural flowing skills.

And the dance continued until the pianist suddenly stopped playing to light a cigarette. Charlie slumped, but the mood persisted.

That night, she danced to perfection, the best she had ever achieved, and occasionally she caught a glimpse of the conductor's face down in the orchestra pit. She saw he was smiling and it encouraged her to greater, more expressive movements. What he knew, but she didn't, was that there was a special member of the audience to see it.

Charlie had caught the eye of a watching producer. Aaron Blomfeld—who had discovered the Songsters writers and staged their big hits *The Age of Romance* and *Doctors and Nurses*—came backstage after the performance to praise her and say she was destined for future success. Four days later, a telephone message left at the stage door asked her to contact his office, and when she did phone, she was asked to come in to discuss a role in his planned new West End production.

That "discussion" was the lead to her invitation to the successful audition.

# Chapter 5

# SHOW TIME

Charlie was in a state of euphoria for a couple of weeks during which nothing happened, but when she did not hear anything, she began to get a few misgivings. She wondered if she should get in touch with the producer or just wait. It was a new experience for her.

The show was called *That Girl Next Door* and was a straight old-fashioned love story about boy and girl neighbours in a block of flats: boy meets girl, boy loses girl, boy and girl reunite for happy-ever-after ending. Even in her wildest dreams Charlie could never have imagined getting a lead role in a West End show so early in her career. *I'm going to be a real gypsy—a dancer*, she thought.

It was the third West End show for Aaron and writers Harry and Danny—and Aaron insisted it would be an even bigger hit than either of the others. *Age*, with its originality, had been London's biggest hit for years and had gone to Broadway, while *Doctors* had already been running in London for over eighteen months and was also due to switch to Broadway. Both had been picked up by Hollywood. Even now, the film of *Age* was awaiting its London opening and the other was in production.

So far, it had all been success for Danny, Harry and Aaron, and now even before their third show was due in London, there was talk of it being transferred to Broadway, and right from the start Aaron had told Charlie that if it did, she would continue her lead role in America. He even indicated that there was talk of a major film deal in the offing, and backed by Aaron's smooth talk Charlie wanted to grab that as well.

But nothing happened until suddenly Aaron phoned her out of the blue to invite her to meet up at a get-together in a private room at a West End restaurant.

"A few of us connected with the show are going to be there—a sort of getting-to-know-you moment," he said, before singing off-key and badly the first lines of the big Rodgers and Hammerstein song "*Getting to Know You*".

Charlie quickly joined in and they both laughed.

As it turned out, the "few of us" included the whole of the cast and crew, almost a hundred people in all.

The director was a big name, Lionel Marsden, who was a bit of a grumpy old man complaining that things were not the same as when he was an up-and-coming hopeful. There was the leading man, Adam, a good-looking, virile young man in his mid-twenties, fractionally taller than Charlie, with a cheery personality and what is commonly called a flashing smile. There was a comedian, Rick Shaw, who had been offered the role as the boy's best friend to provide light relief but who was to prove to be incredible boring off stage and when not performing, and there was another girl, Kate

Gardner, a youngish, prettyish, experienced West End actress who offered Charlie support and, as it turned out, eventually friendship.

Charlie hit it off from the start with Adam and Kate, and they chatted throughout the meal like established, long-standing friends.

"You just don't know what you're letting yourself in for, tying up with Aaron," laughed Adam.

"Ah, but he's the price you have to pay for working with Danny and Harry," added Kate.

"Oo, that Danny. He's dishy," threw in Charlie. "Anyway, Aaron makes me laugh."

They all agreed that Danny and Harry were magical and that they were lucky to be part of their new show.

"But don't forget it's Aaron who pays the cheques," added Adam. "Or anyone he can borrow money from."

Of the three of them, two were complete newcomers to the West End scene, despite Charlie's three-day non-singing turn, with Kate the relatively experienced one with two shows behind her. Charlie and Adam kept asking her if it was as dazzling as it was said to be. Kate said she was still too bewitched, bothered and bewildered by the whole thing to give a coherent answer.

For some reason, those lines from another old song struck Adam and Charlie as funny, and the three of them started to laugh, and laughed all the way through from there on.

The get-together was a huge success that left Aaron smiling and rubbing his hands not only with glee but with the prospect of another hit.

*That Girl Next Door* went into rehearsal on a cold, damp day early in February. With Aaron's record, this time he had been given the actual theatre in which to prepare, and from the first day Lionel, the director, set to work mapping out the staging of each number with Charlie, Adam and the rest of the crew.

From the start, he was insistent that they all stuck to exact reference points during the numbers. The back of the curtain was marked off one to eight on either side of a central line—with one in the centre and eight towards the wings—so they could line up before curtain up, and there were little bits of white tape unseen by the audience as markers on which they had to stand.

Various parts of the stage were also "blocked out" with chalk marks on the floor as an indication to the performers. It all prevented collisions, said Lionel as he told the dancers and crew whether to stand "stage left", which was actually to the right from the audience's point of view, or "stage right".

Lionel was adamant that everyone warmed up thoroughly before each rehearsal or after a break, and he made all the singers keep a jug of water in the wings to keep their voices lubricated.

The set was not built when rehearsals began, but the technicians had mocked-up a rough replica of the leading characters' apartments on stage, designed so that the two flats—the boy's and the girl's—were on either side of the stage, Charlie's at stage level and the boy's opposite and slightly raised. They had to be careful moving around in these "apartments" because there were various coloured lights either attached to scaffolding or hanging from ropes at the back and sides of each and which could easily trip them.

Their voices blended well, even with the echoes because there was no scenery, and with the sound echoing up to the top of the ninety-foot-high stage area, so high that at least one of the electricians who climbed mountains as a hobby had an attack of vertigo when he went up the rigging to adjust some lights on the narrow platform at the top.

The stage area was one of three main zones in the theatre: ninety-foot high by ninety wide and ninety deep. In front of the stage was the auditorium, the front of house, while behind the stage was an equally huge sector used for storage. Spare bits of scenery were kept there which the crew could wheel into position as and when required.

"Why do they call them the crew?" one of the young dancers asked Charlie on the first day of rehearsal.

Charlie didn't know, but stage manager Don Trolley explained that it was because in the early days of London theatres off-duty sailors would come up from the Thames to earn extra money backstage for beer and womanising. "It's also why we call the supports for the lights the rigging," he added.

Danny and Harry, the two writers, had devised a couple of scenes in which Charlie and Adam were seen in their "apartments", singing alternate lines of what appeared to be different songs but that fitted into a perfect "single duet" about what they were both thinking, the sounds melding perfectly.

"You two are a great duet—probably the best since Romeo and Juliet or... or... Marks and Spencer," said Aaron when he heard them sing together for the first time. He pronounced it "doo-et".

There was a particularly romantic song that quickly played a major part in helping Charlie and Adam get along well, and they spent most of their time together. One evening, after a hard day's rehearsing, they went to a small club that Adam had heard about and found there was dancing on a small floor, with a made-up band of drop-in musicians. Charlie recognised one or two from their show. She and Adam danced intimately, and rhythmically.

Rehearsals continued, the pace slowly building up. As well as learning the role, Charlie found she learnt a lot from Harry and Danny; the writer and lyricist were both helpful in the extreme in showing her how to interpret and project their songs. At times, her dancing to some of their wilder songs took on a kind of untamed feral nature that Danny, in particular, applauded.

"I don't know what it is, but you kind of add something to the songs," he told Charlie.

By now, the lyricist's work came naturally and on tap as needed. As a youngster, his instinctive, natural talent had seen him get by, but now he had mastered all the rhymes he had worked so hard to conquer as a young writer. Double or triple rhymes, multiple rhymes, slant rhymes, fragmented rhymes, interior rhymes, feminine rhymes, intricate rhymes, witty rhymes or minor key melodies. All came easily, and by now he had the confidence to use them all.

Sitting to one side during one song rehearsal, Adam asked him why he'd never written a seasonal song for the hit charts.

"Irving Berlin has them all sown up: 'White Christmas', 'Easter Parade'..." grinned Harry, knowing it was a bit of a challenge for Danny.

"Yeah, right," Adam said. "But we're now in mid-winter, how about that?"

Danny hardly paused.

"I know it's coming, the shortest day," he crooned softly. "And I hate the winter solstice. Better fix it soon with a hot warming poultice."

With success, things like that all came quite naturally and easily to him. He could produce words to a new song with confidence in moments, and often did.

One day, when a new song was needed to fill a gap, he remembered a tune that had been cut from their first show because of time restrictions and suggested it. Harry went to the piano and started to play it, and as Charlie automatically started dancing to it, Danny suggested a sort of boogie arrangement with the left hand giving the rhythm for the dancer and the right the melodic grace needed to make it flow. Everyone liked it. It was ideal for Charlie, so Danny went into a corner to get lyrics, and very shortly after came up with a creased bit of paper and handed it over.

"Only rough, but it's an idea," he said.

One of the others muttered about how quick it was, and Harry turned to Charlie. "It's based on an old lead sheet. Some rough old rubbish he drafted to give an idea of the rhythm and flow of another piece. He must have had it in his pocket, and thought it fitted with your dancing."

"I'll do some proper lyrics when I've got time. Polish it up," added Danny.

Charlie and Danny had quickly found themselves on the same wavelength—Danny and Harry were already there—and the team decided to feature the song with Charlie's dance. They had to shuffle some other songs round to accommodate it in a better position in the running order, just before an interval break.

On another occasion, Harry and Danny came in with a jingly, jivey sort of tune that Charlie heard and once again instinctively started to dance to. She made it a mix of ballet leaps and wild taps—a grooving that fitted perfectly.

"We call it 'Jumping Jaguar'," said Danny.

The show's publicist leapt in with, "If we pushed it hard, we could make it the new dance craze, rather like the Black Bottom of the twenties and thirties."

Rehearsals were fun and slightly chaotic when Aaron, the producer, became involved, but it was not all happiness and light. On one rare occasion, Harry complained about the tempo someone used singing one of his songs.

"Oh," said the singer poofily, "You're in a bit of a strop today, aren't you?"

"No," replied Danny. "He's just annoyed 'cause you're singing the vest all wrong."

"What's the vest?" Charlie, who was standing nearby, asked innocently.

"Oh, just something I heard a professional mention somewhere along the line. Nothing for you to worry about," said Danny with a smile.

"Ignore him," said Harry, quickly over his annoyance with the original singer. "It's just those last couple of lines before the chorus and he's not singing it right. But that's not what's bothering me. It's just his general phrasing. It's all wrong. Nothing to do with you though, Charlie. Just ignore it."

Mostly though, the rehearsals went easily and well, and between times, cast and technicians chatted about shows and music, and they were generally a happy bunch. If Harry was a bit introverted though, Danny always took the lead in the talks.

"What comes first: the music or the words?" he was often asked.

"As they always say, first comes the contract," was the inevitable answer everyone knew he would give.

It was Danny and his bubbling, enthusiastic optimism that largely held the rehearsals together. Although mainly friendly, there were occasional rumblings from members of the cast—mixing "straight" actors with dancers and singers wasn't always the best mix.

"Get me a cup of coffee, dearie," said one of the ageing actors to a show girl one afternoon.

"What did your last servant die from?"

"AIDS, actually. Now get me a cup of coffee. Be a love."

"Get it yourself…"

But things generally went well. Charlie enjoyed herself and grew in stature as the rehearsals finally got to their end and the show moved on to a series of try-out shows that went down well.

Then it was on to the big West End opening.

# Chapter 6

# OPENING NIGHT

Opening night seemed to come round quickly—too quickly for Lionel, the director, who always wanted more from his cast.

Charlie had managed to control herself well in the build-up to the night, but now that it had arrived, she was feeling quite nervous. As the orchestra began the overture, she peeked through the heavy stage curtain from the wings, seeing the packed audience in the auditorium then, without a word, she moved to her exactly marked position just off centre stage ready for curtain up. The opening had her alone on stage, a solo act.

It was a dramatic opening with the curtain rising on an apparently empty stage. Charlie was dark against the backdrop so as to be invisible to the audience, then suddenly a single spotlight from a bracket hanging in front of the Royal Circle blinked on catching her full face, with a glint of determination shining from her eyes that the conductor spotted but that the audience could not see. She couldn't see anything with the light in her eyes, but she was eager, sharp, focused—all attention was on her, and as the music hit the note, the spotlight widened to show her in full.

Charlie heard the music. She heard it, felt it, and began to dance and dance, holding the audience spellbound from the start. Just as she had on her sixth birthday.

As she moved to the music, Charlie thrilled to the swish and swirl of her full-skirted costume, delighted to the sequined flashes of the chorus line that had quietly slipped on-stage behind her. Held high by leading man Adam during the number, she felt she was flying, dancing on air.

Adam put her down, and they danced on together—vigorously—then they held a pose as the chorus did a short spell. Charlie and Adam were panting after their particularly strenuous piece, then they both took deep, deep breaths and did another bit of the dance.

In front of her in the auditorium, although Charlie could make out the television screen hanging from the lower balcony showing the orchestra conductor she could only see that there were many round blobs of pink peering through the dark.

Between numbers as she was waiting in the wings backstage, in the middle of one particularly quick change of costume, Charlie heard the show's comedian start a joke to one of the girls, but he had to break off before the end to dash on stage to do a little magic business before he returned to give the punch line.

Then there was the final number, the curtain dropped, and she heard the audience applauding loudly. The curtain went up again, and without exception everyone in the auditorium was standing. The cast took their bows, together and singly—Charlie's was probably the loudest and the audience kept applauding even after the curtain had fallen. The stage manager ordered it up again, and there were more bows.

By now the audience was clapping in rhythm, and Charlie did an extra little jig to accompany them. It went down well. She bowed to the conductor, and noticed for the first time that tonight there was a female trumpeter—very rare.

The reviews the next day were ecstatic: about the show, the songs, the atmosphere, but mostly about Charlie. A new, big star was born, and within days—almost hours it seemed—she was being invited onto all the TV chat shows and was interviewed by the papers. Magazines demanded long feature interviews and photo sessions, and she received invitations to dine at fashionable dinners. Charities scrambled to get her approval.

Charlie took it all in her stride. Everyone backed her, even Adam who realised that all publicity—even that not involving him—was good publicity for the show, and in his favour.

"You're the star. Go for it," he told her, albeit a little grudgingly.

After a couple of weeks of the run, Aaron invited Charlie and Adam to the premiere of the film *The Age of Romance*, an earlier show by songsters Harry and Danny that he'd produced. Because of their own show, the glittering premiere of the film was to be launched in Leicester Square on a Thursday afternoon.

It was a sullen, slightly overcast day with a pale sun flashing on and off like a floodlight as clouds rolled by. Charlie turned up with Aaron, Harry and Danny, driven to the cinema in an ostentatious long limousine that drew up carefully right by the inevitable red carpet. A huge crowd of celebrity gawpers and some cinema and theatre fans ignored the three men but gasped at Charlie's audacious gown.

Despite the boldness of the designer dress, it was tasteful: an elegant dark blue, off one shoulder and quite low at the back. Charlie wore her hair high, and at her neck she had a sparkling diamond necklace that Aaron had rented for the event. She looked every inch a star. At the cinema end of the red carpet, Adam was waiting to present her with a large bouquet of white orchids. Camera lights flashed.

As they walked into the cinema together, the writers and producer accompanied by an anxious PR assistant a few paces behind them, Adam turned his head to look at Charlie.

"This is the real thing, hey, doll?" he said cheerfully, flashing his naturally handsome smile.

Charlie nodded.

"And I bet all the papers say you radiated bright light on a dismal sunless day... with the handsome Adonis next to you lighting up the path ahead of you." This time he flashed his beaming stage smile to indicate he was joking.

Charlie felt that all was well.

The film was good, and the critics approved.

That night Charlie and Adam's dancing on stage was classic. When the long evening show was over, they relaxed in her dressing room, both now in dressing gowns over light underclothing.

"I still feel like dancing," he said.

"Still?"

"Yes. But not the stuff we've been doing. Dancing—you know, arm in arm, cheek to cheek."

"There's no music."

He started to sing, very softly, then held out his arms, and Charlie stood and folded into them. His singing turned to a melodic hum, and they danced slowly, drifting in a haze of music and emotion. It all added up, and Charlie—in a bit of a mental haze—felt she was falling in love with Adam.

Too soon it was over. Charlie blinked, her eyes damp, and Adam suddenly took on a predatory air.

"I've got to get dressed," said Charlie, not quite knowing what to do and feeling just a little scared.

Adam hesitated, noticeably, then nodded. "Yep," he replied, "There's no music…"

After that, Adam carried on with his covetous attraction towards Charlie, and persisted in his chase of her by his words and by touching her hand or shoulder, somehow "accidentally" brushing against her in a more than sensual way while on stage when she could not react. It was a series of slow but insidious actions, and slowly but inevitably she began to weaken towards him.

After an evening performance about a week or so later, he invited her back to his apartment, where she cooked him scrambled eggs.

"A pity you haven't got any baked beans," she said as they sat in his kitchenette eating the snack.

The second-floor apartment had a small balcony, and as it was a balmy evening, they turned out the lights in the large main room and went outside to have an extra glass of wine on it after eating. Sitting on the balcony floor with their backs against the wall, they looked at the myriad lights of London.

It was a magical moment for Charlie, and again she felt she was falling in love. A heady, giddy feeling.

She tried to snuggle close to Adam, but despite his most recent efforts along the same lines, he seemed to edge away from her. She wanted to kiss him, but she didn't have the courage to make the first move.

Finally, at around three in the morning, he stood up. "Better go to bed," he said. "Going to be another hard day tomorrow."

Charlie stood up with him, trying to cuddle close, and as they moved back into the room he pointed to the bedroom. "You take the bed. I'll sleep on the sofa over there."

Charlie was surprised and disappointed, but she didn't say anything. She was at a loss to understand Adam's actions, because she knew—it had been obvious and overt—he had been trying everything he knew to seduce her. His unexpected mood switch was a mystery, and a slap in the face. She didn't sleep well although the double bed was soft and comfortable.

In the morning, she made some toast, which they had with a lemon marmalade she didn't like, then left to go to the theatre for that afternoon's matinee. Adam asked her if she had slept well, but apart from that neither of them said a word.

Days later, Adam had to stay on at the theatre after the evening performance to meet his agent, and so he gave her the keys to his apartment. She went there and, after preparing a meal, stripped off. She was completely nude when he finally arrived, but he ignored her, yawned and said he was going straight to bed—in his own room. Charlie was left alone, a strange feeling of mixed disappointment and hurt filling her mind. As Adam closed his bedroom door, she could only dress and go home. The meal she had prepared stayed uncooked on a table top.

Soon afterwards, a week after a lunch with his agent, Adam decided he wanted to move on, to leave the show. He said he had been offered another part, and felt that as Charlie had won most of the glory in *That Girl Next Door* he wanted more of the spotlight for himself. A young dancer called Peter Mitchener was called in to replace him.

Peter was just a little shorter than Adam—the same height as Charlie to be exact—but he was just as good-looking, as friendly, and much lighter on his feet. He had dark hair, and always wore a white shirt in contrast to the brightly colourful shirts of most of the young dancers, and was generally what is described as "the boy next door". Even though Charlie had found dancing with Adam not too difficult, it was easier with Peter.

She found she didn't miss Adam, and any feelings she might have had towards him disappeared as she threw herself into working whole-heartedly for the show. She was invariably first to the theatre and would often sit having a cup of tea with the stage door keeper in his small "office" until the rest of the cast and crew arrived.

Charlie and Peter worked well together, and after a run of just over a year Aaron decided to move them as a team to his new show —a fourth by writers Harry and Danny called *My Love*.

"I've got a hunch in my water that you two are going to take the West End by storm again," Aaron told them. "Hey, listen t' that: in my water, a storm. Hee hee."

He started to cough, spluttering a little. When he recovered, he went on. "Broadway too, maybe. Like the Astaires way back. Remember, Fred and his sister whose name I've forgotten. They were partners both sides of the Atlantic." He coughed again. "And in Hollywood."

Peter didn't think Adele Astaire had ever danced with Fred in a film, but he didn't say anything.

By now, Aaron was finding it easier to raise backing. He, Harry and Danny were on a success roll, and on top of that Charlie's name alone was by now enough to ensure good bookings. It meant that things moved swiftly, and in what was near record time, *My Love* was set up and in rehearsal.

# Chapter 7

# ROMANCE

At first only the four lead characters of *My Love* met in a rehearsal studio in the West End, and Charlie kept the habit of being first to arrive—even when after a surprisingly short two and a half weeks the lesser characters were brought in, before they all moved to a larger rehearsal studio a few streets away in Old Compton Street.

It was there that a few of the musicians hired to form the basis of the theatre orchestra were also called in to set the music for the dancers' practice and the real hard work of preparing a musical began. Harry and Danny were always on hand to adapt their songs as needed, and things really began to swing.

Charlie, in particular, got on well with the musicians—despite Peter's obvious, sneering self-superiority over them—and in particular she liked a young-looking trumpeter called Lou Bainbridge. He was traditionally good-looking with slicked back black hair, a slightly retroussé nose, piercing dark brown, almost black, eyes, and an almost permanent smile that often exploded into infectious laughter. His parents had named him after their favourite, Louis Armstrong.

After just a couple of days, during which Charlie often managed to join in his friendly school boy teasing of his fellow musicians, she got to the mirror-lined rehearsal room early as usual, and was just beginning her usual warm-up routine—still wearing her street coat as the room was cold—when Lou also arrived. It was remarkably early and out of character for him, but they chatted aimlessly but easily together.

Then, as the rest of the dancers, musicians and crew were due to arrive, Lou asked Charlie if she would like to go for a drink to relax after what they both knew would be a hard day's rehearsal. She was surprised but pleased and instantly agreed, and when the session ended, they went off together to a bar he knew in Flitcroft Street, right in the heart of London's Tin Pan Alley.

The bar was called Out of Tune, and was used almost exclusively by musicians relaxing after long playing sessions of their differing kinds of music and well into the night. Lou was well known there, and was greeted by many of the staff and other customers as he and Charlie walked in out of the evening sunshine into its half-light interior.

After a couple of drinks during which he was constantly interrupted by friends wanting to talk about various gigs they had enjoyed together or gossip about upcoming jobs, Lou suggested they move on and took Charlie to a small French restaurant he knew in Denmark Street, the real heart of show biz.

He was equally well known there, and after an enjoyable meal accompanied by across-the-restaurant banter with the proprietor and his wife, Charlie said she had to get home.

"If I stay here much longer, I'll be here all night. And I've got to get some sleep before rehearsals tomorrow," she said.

Lou agreed, and they parted in good spirits as he called for a taxi to take her home.

Charlie enjoyed the evening, and readily agreed to a follow-up date after the schedules promised hectic and tiring rehearsals the next day.

It was raining the next morning and the weather threw a bit of a pall over rehearsals, but despite that Charlie and Peter worked well, responding eagerly to Aaron's regular choreographer Eddie Martin's ideas and director Lionel Marsden's suggestions.

The day went by quickly, and when rehearsals broke at around 3:30, the sun was shining, and Charlie and Lou left the rehearsal room together. Outside, Lou called for a taxi and, without a word, got it to take them to the Out of Tune bar.

The bar was empty, so they had one quick drink before Lou suggested going to see a filmed version of a big West End musical at a local cinema.

Sitting in the dark, Lou unobtrusively held Charlie's hand loosely, and she nestled towards him in their cosy cinema seats. He seemed slightly disinterested in the film, but Charlie had a strong desire to dance the numbers along with the characters on the large screen in front of them.

After a couple of hours, the film ended and they went off to a cafe, where Charlie spoke enthusiastically about the film they had just seen, and Lou nodded and agreed. After half an hour or so, at

Lou's suggestion, they returned to Out of Tune. This time it was Lou who became livelier, while Charlie just sat at a table listening to him and his friends jazzing away.

At around ten, she told him she had to get home to rest before the next day's early morning rehearsal call. He took her outside, called for a taxi and, when it arrived, gave the driver her address and a bank note. He opened the door for Charlie before pulling her towards him and kissing her full on the lips with feeling. As the taxi moved off, he went back into the bar.

Lou was not on call the next day, but he had arranged to meet Charlie at the pub at seven. When she got there, he was standing at the bar chatting to a group of friends, unshaven and looking a bit dishevelled. Charlie got the impression that he could have been in the bar all night.

As Charlie came up, the others were laughing, but Lou heard her and turned to look at her.

"Help, babe," he said. "Come and meet some friends of mine."

The evening passed very quickly in a blur of musical jokes, reminiscences of past concerts and shows, and a lot of laughter.

In the days that followed, Charlie and Lou had a lot of fun together. They rehearsed hard during the day, and in the evenings went for meals, to cinemas and other theatres. Life was full and lively, and kissing became a regular habit, and the only thing to mar it from Charlie's point of view was that when she said she wanted to go dancing, Lou refused, saying with a laugh, "I don't like dancing, only dancers—particularly long-legged ones."

Despite that, they had fun, and it wasn't too long before Charlie was staying the night at Lou's flat in West Hampstead at least three days a week. It was very untidy and, although naturally neat herself, she accepted it at first.

After a few visits, Lou gave Charlie a key of her own, and when she had an afternoon off while he was at a band rehearsal, she spent two hours cleaning it up: hanging Lou's clothes in cupboards, putting everything into its rightful place, and even mopping and vacuuming the floors and carpets. When Lou arrived home, he didn't say anything about the new tidy apartment, but when Charlie returned three days later, his clothes were again strewn around and everything was as untidy as before.

Charlie accepted it as she slowly began to realise that, once again, she was falling in love. She enjoyed her time with Lou, although the one thing that upset her was that Lou always seemed more interested when he took her to jazz clubs and left her while he went to sit in on a set with the other casual musicians he met there.

Things continued at what seemed a frenetic pace—Charlie was busy rehearsing, always dancing with energy and zest, and then going around late into the night with Lou. She always ended up exhausted at the end of the day, but found renewed energy when rehearsals started the next morning. Life was good.

As opening night got near, there was the added pressure of newspaper and television interviews, and Charlie had to give up occasional evenings with Lou as she scrambled from TV or radio studio to a bar somewhere in the West End to meet a reporter or news photographer. She managed well, although it was hard work repeating the same answers to the same questions time after time, always trying to put a new slant on things, but in her mind always with the basic idea of "selling" the show rather than herself. Sometimes Peter was with her on chat shows or during the interviews, but he always seemed more intent on putting himself across as a star.

All the time she was having a whirl with Lou, falling more in love with him although he didn't seem bothered by the fact she was so busy. He continued to take her to music clubs or just drinking with his musician friends in Out of Tune.

Eventually, Charlie had to slow down as Aaron arranged a series of settling-in shows before invited audiences leading up to the opening night of *My Love*.

Then the show opened—the now inevitable success for writers Harry and Danny—and life for Charlie settled down to a round of matinees, evening shows, occasional updates to dialogue (once even a new song) and she was as happy as she had ever been. After all, there was almost continual dancing and, with the routine, more time to be with Lou.

*My Love* ran to packed houses for several months before Aaron, in what was to prove a master stroke, decided to move Charlie and Peter together into yet another production of his old hit, a revival of *The Age of Romance*, but this time on Broadway. His regular choreographer Eddie and director Lionel were also set to move across the Atlantic.

Although they had played the parts before, there was a need for Charlie and Peter to rehearse before they could move on to the new show, which was adapted for American audiences. Harry and Danny had written a couple of new songs for them, there were new dance routines to learn, and the other senior members of the new cast had to learn to live and work with them.

With their current show and the extra rehearsals for *Ages*, there was little time for Charlie to spend with Lou. He began to get grumpy, and there was a definite cooling between them.

Then the London run of *My Love* ended, and as the curtain finally fell on the final show of the final night, Peter stepped in front of the whole cast lined up on the stage and waited for the on-going applause to finally die down before beginning to make a farewell speech. In a practised voice he feigned sincerity, pretended an embarrassed stutter, and performed the words in a way that defined unctuous.

After paying a fulsome tribute to "my talented and humbling super co-star", he hurried off-stage, one hand close to an eye in mock sincerity until he got into the wings. Out of sight of the audience, he pushed past everyone backstage and went to his dressing room before leaving the theatre as quickly as he could. He did not speak to Charlie.

Aaron had arranged a party in the upstairs room of a famous London restaurant, and although everyone connected with the show was invited, Peter did not turn up. He seemed to be the only one, but Charlie noticed that Lou was not there either. She slipped away after three-quarters of an hour to phone him, but there was no reply from either his apartment nor his mobile.

She debated whether or not to ring Out of Tune, but decided not to and returned to the party intent on having a good time.

# Chapter 8

# BROADWAY

**A**aron had noted Peter's failure to turn up to the farewell party for *My Love* and felt insulted. In a huge fit of pique, he rang Peter's agent and cancelled his contract for Broadway.

By now, he felt he was big enough in the business to take such an action, as after the success of his first few shows he had now assumed the airs and manners of a rich, successful theatrical producer. He acknowledged, at least to himself, that the part the Songsters Harry and Danny had played in his success could not be discounted—he basked in the fact that he had been "the genius" who discovered them and given them their chance. At least, that's what he told everyone.

He had by now begun to dress better—he had always been immaculate in a shabby way—and he smoked better, more expensive cigars less frequently, and his speech improved. By now, he was relatively successful after a couple of long West End runs, and he had deliberately made himself stop the nervous laughter that had punctuated his speech and slowly forced himself to give up repeating the sentences other people threw at him.

He had a "proper" secretary rather than his sour-faced wife—who now wore a fur coat no matter what the weather—and had moved to a larger office on Shaftesbury Avenue. Success had made Aaron become more of a man of substance.

A few days after getting rid of Peter, Aaron flew to New York with Charlie and the rest of his team, where on the recommendation of a fellow producer he knew, he hired a new unknown young American singer Ben Scott to take over the part unseen, explaining that he felt having "a Yank" would help ticket sales.

"You're going to a big star," he told Ben. And with a flash of the old Aaron, he added, "Leave it to me. I'll fix it before you can say Jack Rubenstein."

Ben was younger than Charlie and inexperienced, and when they met in an up-town office, he listened to every small bit of advice she and the others gave him. Charlie took an instant liking to him.

The day before rehearsals were due to begin, Aaron arranged for the cast to look round his chosen theatre: the New Amsterdam on West 42nd Street between 7th and 8th Avenues. The theatre was dark and waiting for *Age* to come in, and for Charlie it was a thrill because she knew the theatre had been the home of all the big, opulent musicals put on by the legendary impresario Florenz Ziegfeld at the turn of the twentieth century and into the dazzling 1930s.

They got a minibus to take them, and as it stopped in front of the tall theatre—already with the name of the show and with Charlie and Ben's names listed in turned-off lights above the entrance—Charlie couldn't help muttering, "Charlene, you're going out an English youngster, but you're going to come back a Broadway star."

It was an adaptation of the famous line from the play *42nd Street*, and she said it in a phoney accentuated Brooklyn accent, a huge smile on her happy face.

The guide on the tour of the empty theatre told them that it had opened in 1903 and had promptly been dubbed as "The House Beautiful", and as they entered by the sumptuous front entrance Charlie could see why as she looked round the foyer at the marble wall sculptures showing moments from great Shakespearean plays and scenes from Wagner's Ring Cycle operas.

The theme continued as they walked through the corridors into the auditorium, where more Shakespearean characters blended with literary figures from Hans Christian Anderson, Aesop and some classic myths. Her mouth literally dropped open, and she stood in amazed awe as, away to the right, she saw figures of the great stars who had graced the stage in "the old days"—people like Will Rogers, W. C. Fields, Fanny Bryce and Eddie Cantor. Watching over them, she saw Ziegfeld himself.

Ziegfeld, the guide told them, opened Follies in June of 1913, and for the next fourteen years they were synonymous with "The House Beautiful", featuring spectacular sets, lavish costumes and the biggest stars of the day. The main attraction was, he added, the long line of beautiful chorus girls hand-picked by Ziegfeld himself to ornament those spectacular shows. Their glamour, high-kicking and dancing were a forerunner of everything Aaron, Harry and Danny had tried to recreate in all their shows.

Charlie almost whispered as she spoke to Aaron, "I hope we can live up to all this."

As they were walking round, Aaron got a call on his mobile, and while they waited for him, Charlie spoke to one of the security men hovering nearby. She lapped it up as he told her the theatre had a ghost—a famous ghost of a former chorus girl who had starred in many of the Ziegfeld Follies.

Olive Thomas, he explained, was a former Follies chorus girl, a sister to the first big silent screen film star Mary Pickford, who had been haunting the theatre since her mysterious death from poisoning in 1920, although it is still not known whether that was an accident, suicide... or even murder.

"Most people who've said they've seen the ghost say they saw her running across the stage blowing kisses to the audience, even when the theatre's empty," he said.

Several others had gathered round him and Charlie as he went on. "It's not only in old times. She's made appearances in recent times too. Many of the house staff and overnight security people have often said they've felt a touch on the back, and when they turned round no one was there."

He paused for effect, then went on. "She appears so often we've got photos of her at every entrance, so us workers can greet her when we arrive for work each day. A lot of us blow her a kiss or touch the picture as we come in or go out, to stop her messing us about on the day. She's got a cracked sense of humour!"

Aaron came back, and the guide became more formal again. But Charlie promised him that she would either blow a kiss or touch Olive's picture every day once the new show opened.

The next day, *The Age of Romance* went into rehearsal. Ben proved to be very talented, and he and Charlie hit it off from the start. There seemed to be a touch of magic when they danced, sang or played scenes together.

The emphasis was on bringing Ben and the new local dancers up to scratch as Charlie had played the part so many times before, and they were largely restricted to mornings only. That meant that as rehearsals took place, Charlie had free time and was able to explore the city, and in particular the Broadway area. Sometimes with Ben, with girls of the chorus—most were New Yorkers and had seen the sights—but more often on her own.

Because no one knew how long they were going to stay in New York—the way the Big Apple took to the show and the length of its run made it a case of guesswork despite Aaron's natural optimism— Charlie had been moved into a small, cheap hotel near the theatre rather than renting an exorbitantly expensive house.

Within a day or two, she began exploring the district, starting off with the area close to the theatre. She visited the world famous Times Square—named after the New York Times paper that used to be headquartered there and which is now the heart of Theatreland in New York—at night, marvelling at the huge multitude of neon signs and lights that made it known as the Great White Way, and on other days she toured the non-theatrical parts of the city like the Statue of Liberty, Central Park, the Empire State building—she went to the top floor—and even Harlem.

Then she found Hell's Kitchen.

Although she didn't feel at all stagey or anything like that, she revelled in Hell's Kitchen, a neighbourhood on the west side of Manhattan, close to Theatreland and packed with restaurants and cheapish accommodation which is regarded as the natural New York home for stage people, particularly young, hopeful actors, including those enrolled at the famous Actors Studio, where method acting was born.

Charlie loved her food—the energy she used in her daily routine of rehearsing and dancing gave her a big, healthy appetite—so she found the area delightful, with restaurants providing food from countries around the world. She quickly discovered Restaurant Row on West 46th Street, and as time went on spent a lot of time at the Ninth Avenue Association's International Food Festival, one of the oldest street fairs in the city with a dozen different ethnic foods to choose from, with Indian restaurants vying with others from Afghan, Argentine, Ethiopia, Peru, Turkey, India, Pakistan and Vietnam.

With Aaron's permission, she moved to another small hotel close to the theatre, and later, after the show had opened and she was often called in to guest on radio and TV shows, she was glad that she was staying near the many studios in the area.

Charlie saw all the traditional sights of New York: Broadway at night was an explosion of light, the Brooklyn Bridge, the World Trade Center and Grand Central Station. She took the ferry to Liberty Island, with the Statue of Liberty and its unforgettable view of the New York skyline, and she saw the Woolworth Building, St. Patrick's Cathedral and Columbus Circle, and she went walking—in daylight, of course—in Central Park. In more sombre moments, she visited the 9/11 Museum and the John Lennon memorial.

She went to 1 Shubert Alley, a shop in the cut-through between 44th and 45th Streets and next door to the Booth Theatre—the shop used to be one of the theatre's star dressing rooms—to buy souvenirs for friends and relatives back home, and she also got expensive baseball caps, mugs and everything that supposedly showed off Broadway for the members of the show's cast, orchestra and crew.

But most of her attention was, naturally, on the show and when she got bored with sight-seeing, she attended rehearsals even on her days off.

The rehearsals were a week and a half along when she went back, and were much the same as in England, although they were far more relaxed. They took place in a room on the sixteenth floor of a skyscraper on 8th Avenue, two sides complete with floor-to-ceiling mirrors and the usual barre bars and the other two full-length windows with a view of the Empire State Building.

When the crew was together up there, it was nothing like the scene that audiences would eventually see—there was no glitz or glamour. Just a lot of sweat. After two days blocking out the movements, choreographer Eddie was getting things together in a brisk fashion under the watchful eye of director Lionel. Everyone worked very hard, willingly.

Charlie watched it all with interest, happy with everything Eddie did, but she did not interfere although she chatted to Eddie frequently.

"You're working the boys and girls very hard," she commented one day during a short rest.

"Yes, it's shit…" replied Eddie.

Charlie looked puzzled.

Eddie laughed. "SHIT: Special High Intensity Training," he explained.

When they were rehearsing, the dancers all had tight-fitting clothes for ease of movement, while the singers and musicians wore their everyday clothes: jeans, loose T-shirts—some with weird or obscene messages on the front—and sneakers.

The bandsmen looked slightly out of place sitting in formal semi-circular lines and playing in unison. But the music flowed—and swayed—and was lyrical. It made you want to dance, even if you were not directly involved. Charlie lapped up the atmosphere. New York was forgotten—this was what she wanted.

The Broadway opening of *Age* was a night of razz-a-ma-tazz. Searchlights stabbed the sky over Broadway, 42nd Street and Times Square, bathing the large crowds that always gathered for "an event" in an artificial, brighter than daylight light. An hour before the show was due to start, things on the streets had reached a high peak of intoxicated titillation and exhilaration.

Before the opening, celebrities preened and posed on the traditional red carpet on their way into the theatre, and once inside spent time before curtain-up looking round at everyone else, all of them trying to be noticed.

Stage manager Macky McIntire gave precise orders, then contradicted each and every one with no one taking any notice. The crew knew exactly what they had to do and did it.

Charlie, Ben and the others were either alone in their rooms or in the communal chorus dressing room putting on make-up, costumes and doing their individual muscle and voice warm-ups. They were all fighting an inward excitement, trying to keep calm and concentrate on the work they were about to begin.

They had all been at the theatre for more than an hour and a half, and now the call finally came from stage side for the first of them to step forwards.

"Charlie, Ben, beginners please," called someone, and Charlie and Ben made their way to the wings with the chorus.

"Break a leg," she said—the traditional good luck wish in theatres.

Ben grinned. "You too," he replied.

Everything was ready. The orchestra, under the ornate proscenium arch between the first row of the stalls and the stage apron, had stopped tuning up and waited for conductor Mathew Wallace to give them the signal. As he got the cue over his headphones from the prompt box in the wings at stage left, he lifted both hands, paused for a second, then pointing at the violin section, started to slowly give the rhythm.

Danny and Harry, standing in the wings, heard clips of the music they had created and heard so many times before and began to breathe deeply and slowly. Then the curtain started to lift—*The Age of Romance* began its Broadway run.

The show went as planned and precisely rehearsed, and the audience, apart from applauding odd bits of music, singing or dancing, was silent and enthralled. Everything fitted into place and things went smoothly.

And then the show was over. The curtain dropped and the audience rose in unison in a cacophonous roar of applause, cheering, whooping and whistling. Behind the curtain, a perspiring Charlie stood with Ben and the others in a long row, breathing deeply but with smiles spreading from one to another as they heard the muffled response from the audience.

The curtain rose again, and they took their bows—together and individually. Charlie and Ben were called forward ten times, then Charlie took a further seven solo curtain calls before the curtain came down for the final time that night. Suddenly, everyone was laughing and talking. There were hugs and kisses all round—they all knew they had a hit on their hands. For Charlie and Ben, it was the thrill of success. For the crew and chorus girls, it was the promise of wages for a long time.

After half an hour or so, in which they all stood round furiously chattering breathlessly, eagerly and frantically about nothing, Aaron turned up. He had the widest smile anyone had ever seen, and he was ebulliently telling anyone who would listen about the audience's comments and reactions as they left the theatre.

As the impromptu gathering started to drift away, he asked Charlie, Ben and other leading members of the cast and senior crew to join him for what he described as "a traditional meet" at Sardi's restaurant, about two minutes' walk away on West 44th Street.

It was where most show people went after Broadway openings in the old days, waiting for the morning newspapers to see what the critics had to say. By the time Charlie and the others had changed to their street clothes and gathered at the plush restaurant though, those reviews were already on modern social media.

Aaron had prebooked a private room and had ordered a succulent meal, and although everyone was anxious to look at their mobiles to see what the critics had said—but had so far been busy celebrating or had just forgotten to look—he made them sit down so he could read the reviews out to everyone in one go. He made certain that he had Charlie on his right and Ben on the left before he began.

The reviews could only be described as "raves". They were unanimous and ebullient, enthusiastic and garrulous, in their words over the Songsters' show, and particularly about Charlie, described by one as the new Queen of Broadway. Everyone at the table stood and applauded as Aaron read that out, Ben pretending to doff a cap and bowing low in Charlie's direction.

Despite Aaron's attempts to make her, Charlie refused to make a speech.

"Tonight belongs to all of us," she said, blushing as she realised it was a cliche.

Things finally settled down, and everyone suddenly realised how hungry they were and set out to eat their smoked salmon with multi-grain bread and steaks or jumbo crab cakes, carrying on their happy, jubilant chat. At one point, Eddie started to talk to Charlie about dancing, but she only wanted to dance, not talk about it. Danny, seeing the incident, interrupted and took over the conversation with a series of risqué and downright dirty stories.

It was almost two o'clock when Charlie said she felt exhausted and left the celebration—one of the first to go.

She took a taxi back to her hotel room in Hell's Kitchen to phone Lou. Once again, there was no answer from his phone, although she knew the time in England was only four hours behind her, by now around 11 p.m. in London, and he would have known she was likely to call after her Broadway debut. He should have been there. Despite the disappointment, Charlie went to bed in a happy mood and promptly fell into a deep sleep.

# Chapter 9

To begin with, Charlie had tried many of the small restaurants in the show-bizzy Hell's Kitchen, spreading from 34th Street to 59th Street north to south and 8th Avenue to the Hudson River, but as *Age* settled down to a longish run, she settled into a routine where she, Danny, Harry or Ben—in any combination—would have a pre-show grill at the Hourglass Tavern, would dine at the Taladwat Thai restaurant, drink at l'Argot wine bar, or eat the more familiar Italian dishes at the Amarone bistro. They loved experimenting with different styles of food, especially the more unusual dishes from the Caribbean or Mexico.

By now, Aaron was taking a self-indulgent hedonistic delight with the dreamt-of riches of a successful international theatre producer, and with what was, for him, plenty of money, he would sometimes treat one or a group of actors or dancers to a lavish dinner at the opulent Chez Josephine—"where the legend of Josephine Baker, the great cabaret jazz singer, lives on". He particularly liked the expensive lobster cassoulet there.

Aaron was cute enough to know that the continuing run of *Age* and the continuing high income he derived from it depended to a large extent on Charlie. So, soon after the successful opening, he paid—out of the show accounts—for her to move to a bigger hotel, a small suite in the more luxurious Hampton Inn on 41st Street, just a few minutes stroll from the theatre. Charlie had liked her original stay in the small hotel in Hell's Kitchen, but was quite pleased with the move as it was even closer to the theatre and involved less travel on the subway or bus or a tiring half-hour walk battling with hordes of unseeing New Yorkers.

Apart from the boost to her career, Broadway was completely different—a break from the consecutive long West End runs she had played. It was not that she got bored with the daily repeat as so many other actors and actresses did in a long run, because she was always able to add little nuances to her dances. That made them seem different to her although audiences hardly noticed them, but the move was a welcome change in routine nevertheless.

In many ways, New York was a more exciting city than London, and Charlie absorbed the energy and let loose when she was on stage. If it were possible, her performances got even livelier, and she literally had the whole world at her feet.

There were also the continual extra rehearsals to fit in new danc-ers—many got pregnant during the run and had to leave—and al-though she loved it, Charlie was always exhausted by the time she got back to her apartment. She slept well—deeply and innocently.

At first, she tried phoning Ben every day, but he was rarely at home, and the time difference meant she couldn't try him from the theatre. It upset her, but slowly the feeling faltered, slowed, then began to fade. She realised she had fallen out of love with Ben and concentrated even more on the show—slowly adapting her style slightly to meet the differing demands of American audiences.

The show settled down, with the almost daily good news items, articles and acclaim continuing, and Charlie was in great demand by journalists and TV chat producers.

Despite her growing partnership with Ben, she was—as she had been with Adam and Peter—still the prominent partner, and her star status grew. It didn't seem to affect her. It was, therefore, no real surprise to anyone but her when, after one matinee performance had finished, Aaron, who had flown back to England, rang her at the stage door—"At transatlantic rates!"—to tell her she had been selected for the Royal Variety show in London. The Queen of Broadway had been invited to meet the queen of England.

# Chapter 10

# ROYAL VARIETY

Three days before the Royal Variety show was due to be staged, Charlie flew home to London where the show was to take place at the famous London Palladium.

She met a few of her fellow stars in a bare rehearsal room, but most of those she did meet were disinterested in anyone but themselves, so Charlie concentrated on working up her own act with director Hal Warren, show choreographer Hetty Baron, her Broadway choreographer Eddie—who had accompanied her back to London—and a hand-picked group of long-legged chorus girls. Things went smoothly.

On the night of the show itself, Charlie was taken to a dressing room high up in the theatre, where she put on her costume and tried to quieten her nerves by sitting on an aged and uncomfortable settee rather than watching the other performers. After what seemed like ages, but was in fact just over half an hour, she was called to ready herself for her turn and went down to wait in the wings.

An internationally famous operatic tenor was on stage giving it his all—romantic, melodic, semi-classical—with all the surging rhythms of a full string orchestral backing on stage with him. As she waited in the wings for him to finish, the music began building to a climax. Charlie listened for a moment, then without really think-ing started to dance round the bare space behind the floodlights just off-stage. A stage manager rushed forwards to stop her, but she grabbed him and made him do a few twirls with her. The song ended, and as the compere moved on-stage, the tenor walked off to huge applause, and before returning for his bow, he gave her a huge smile and a big Italianate wink.

"There, I've done your warm-up. Go out there and wow them like you always do," he said in a heavy accent as he returned larger-than-life to the footlights.

Charlie did just that. Her routine was a flamboyant mix of ballet, tap and show biz, and she whizzed and turned round the stage in dazzling flashes of movement—sometimes energetic, sometimes earthy, sometimes gentle.

When she began dancing, she could feel herself flying, her body swaying to the subtle rhythms her body picked out in the melo-dy, feeling the music and adjusting her movements in a whirl of busyness. She loved it all; to her, every time she danced was a new opening night, live with a different audience.

Her pale blue ball gown whirled round as she used the whole stage, occasionally picking out one of the male backing dancers dressed in white top hats and tails to help her with a leap. It was a triumph, and the tenor was waiting in the wings as she came off to give her a bear-like hug.

The Royal Variety show was not like a normal performance. There was something even more star-spangled about it. Alongside the international performers, Charlie felt an especial pride, and as she finished her dance and curtsied towards the Royal Box, she felt she got a personal look of appreciation.

Surprisingly, as she was put into position for the cast line-up backstage at the end of the show she saw the sovereign getting closer, she felt a touch of apprehension in case she should say the wrong thing. When it was her turn, the monarch and the princes and other members of 'The Firm' spoke to her with smiles, but she could not later remember what any of them had said, nor her reply. The curtsies and short exchanges of words passed her in a blur.

Straight after the Royal Variety show, Charlie flew back to New York to pick up her Broadway role. But as she got back to her hotel a severe attack of desynchronisation hit her: jet lag. Switching back to UK time had been swallowed up by the excitement and adrenaline of the rehearsal and actual performance of the show, but back in New York, after four days, she got what seemed to be a double whammy. Literally within hours, the hectic pace of simply living in the Big Apple began to tire her more than usual.

Aaron was fatherly, and although he still occasionally reverted to his old giggling and malapropism ways, he had matured a lot since Charlie had first met him. She had no problem with being open with him and telling him just how exhausted she was. He was understanding and gave her the rest of the week off.

The time off did her good, because when she returned to *Age* on the following Monday she felt as eager and enthusiastic as she had on opening night—boosted, when she arrived at the theatre on Monday, to be surrounded by Ben and the rest of the cast and crew eager to hear her stories of the London Royal Variety show.

Everything quickly became hectic again. Charlie returned to take up her new life without fuss, although a huge horde of agents, PR teams, managers, social media consultants and general "helpers and advisors" started pestering her. She refused all offers of their so-called help, relying on Aaron and the friendliness of Harry and Danny.

Only one offer by someone who described herself as a personal dressmaker even slightly appealed to her, and she asked Danny for his advice. She didn't know why she asked him. He was generally untidy, but he had always been friendly, light-hearted and easy to talk to. Her appeal for help just burst out one day.

"Let's talk about it," he said, and on his suggestion, they went for lunch at Andre's Bakery on 2nd Avenue—the Budapest-style restaurant serving Hungarian food.

"I'm Hungary," he said in his jocular manner as the menu was put before them.

True to his comment, Danny tucked into a huge portion of chicken paprikash with nokedli, which turned out to be a stew with sour cream and handmade noodles, while Charlie simply had an appetising platter of Hungarian salami, sausage, ham and cheese. Danny wanted to eat first, but Charlie only wanted an answer to her problem and left most of her food on the plate.

When Danny had finished twirling the last of his noodles and the meal was over, he simply told her, "Forget her," without another word. They went back to the theatre, and Charlie did just that.

The show continued to run to packed houses, often with standing room around the back of the stalls, and the daily applause and standing ovations were as high as ever. Charlie, especially, lapped it all up although it was such hard work.

# Chapter 11

# FILM TIME

The run on Broadway lasted another fourteen and a half months before Charlie finally decided to call it a day. She was having breakfast one morning when it suddenly occurred to her that she hadn't heard a word from Lou for the best part of a year. Somehow, she hadn't realised it before—or worried about it even on her short trip to England for the Royal Variety show.

When it suddenly came to her though, it suddenly made her think more deeply about home, and she began to feel unsettled and nostalgic. She tried to put the mood into isolation in her mind, but over the next few weeks the feeling built up until she finally decided she really wanted, indeed needed, to return home.

After a few days, she told Aaron, and although it was a blow to him, he accepted that "his" star needed to move on. Charlie said she would continue in the part until her replacement had trained up.

She suggested that one of the chorus girls, Carole Goddard—a long-legged blonde with long curly hair and a pretty oval-shaped face—could be the girl to replace her.

"If you watch her, she's far too good to be a chorine," she told the producer.

Aaron promised to give the girl a trial, and suggested it to Harry, Danny and director Lionel. Choreographer Eddie was also asked his opinion. A trial was organised, and although she was terrified at the thought, Carole impressed. Charlie had decided it would not be right to be at the audition, but she was quickly on the phone to find that Aaron had decided to promote her.

It meant even more extra rehearsals for the cast—with Charlie along to help Carole move up the several grades—and when everyone agreed she was ready, a date was finally fixed for her to take over.

Almost immediately after the switch, Charlie packed up, said her farewells, and flew home with relief. After New York, her plan was to take a long break, and back in England she let it be known that she was officially "resting"—show people slang for someone without a job.

She was glad of the opportunity to rest, but without the intense daily physical effort, the aches and pains she had been feeling throughout her body increased. In particular, the pain in her left knee felt bad. It had been hurting quite badly during her last couple of months in New York, but by now it was quite noticeable. At first, she just thought it was a result of her hard work on *Age* and she didn't do anything about it, hoping the pain would go away.

And it did. After two weeks or so, the knee settled down and Charlie only noticed it occasionally. She hoped she could settle down to "resting".

But it didn't exactly work out like that. Ironically, it was soon after she arrived home that, despite her protests, she became involved in a series of TV chat shows and newspaper or magazine interviews. Most of them were routine, and Charlie sailed through them without any problems—always smiling and "acting out" jollity no matter how bored she was with the seemingly never-ending repeats of the same questions.

There were a few that were not so simple, however. One TV interviewer tried asking about her "affair" with Broadway co-star Ben, and Charlie had to fight down her anger as she denied there had been anything personal between them. It made her pause and hesitate both between and in mid-sentence, and she seemed as if she was having trouble putting her words together. The interviewer smirked and preened, giving "knowing" looks into the camera, and gave the impression that he didn't believe her because in her anger she sounded as if she was trying to cover up. After that, many other interviewers brought the subject up again, but Charlie had learnt her lesson and her answers were always calm, polite and unbelieved—although they were true.

Although she always insisted that she only wanted to talk of matters such as working with Danny and Harry, who she always called The Songsters, and the shows of theirs she had appeared in, the subject was continually, and nauseatingly from her point of view, raised. Charlie finally gave up accepting offers and invitations to give interviews.

On one of the final shows before she stopped, however, she appeared on a television programme about dancing—and it was there that she met and was invited to lunch by celebrated Hollywood film producer, Benjamin A. Thomas.

Despite a string of Oscar-winning and -nominated films, Benjamin was irrelevantly known to all who worked for him as Batty because of his initials, although lesser mortals did not dare call him that to his face. It was a nickname he had fostered, but he far from lived up to it and was indeed a really astute operator.

Batty was a tall, bronzed, broad-shouldered, healthy-looking American with a shock of pure white hair. As on the television show, he dressed smart-casual, and he took Charlie to a restaurant just off Covent Garden, where their table was in a small niche that allowed them to see others but be in a certain amount of privacy while they chatted. Batty spoke intelligently about all manner of things, but Charlie was most fascinated by his tales of his early days trying to make it as a stage producer before then moving into films.

"I got into movies by luck," he told her. "I was running a show off Broadway when they wanted the star in Hollywood. He didn't really want to go, but to try and put 'em off said he would if they took me along as well. They took him at his word. And then, well, I kinda liked the sunshine on the west coast and stayed."

Batty was easy company, and during the meal Charlie light-heartedly suggested that she would love to do an old Fred Astaire style musical film. Batty nodded in agreement.

"Yep, me too," he chuckled. "It's about time the movies returned to the old romantic days. It's all too wham, bang, videos and sex these days. OK for the kids, I suppose, but for my money, romance is the thing. Like you said, a new Astaire–Rogers style movie would be great. Those two... well, they've got to be the best ever."

Despite his big grin and greater knowledge of films, Charlie argued. "I didn't say Astaire and Rogers," she insisted, a big beam on her face. "Personally, I always thought Cyd Charisse was the better dancer and a better partner for Astaire. Their 'Dancing in the Dark' scene in... what was it... *The Band Wagon*? Well, that was just magical. The best."

As she said it, in her mind she recalled her own near start of a romantic "Dancing in the Dark" dressing room episode with her first West End partner, Adam Knowles.

Batty woke her from her momentary mental dream. "OK, OK, but Fred and Ging had a certain something that hit at the box office like no one else," he told her.

"But do you think anyone remembers them?"

Batty smiled benevolently. "Yep. I'm a producer and it's important for me to know things like that! Trouble is, although I think the public would love to see that kind of movie, the money men don't. End of."

After lunch, the two of them wandered out into Covent Garden. There was a lively, people-filled atmosphere in the air, but suddenly Batty said he was starting to feel tired. He hailed a taxi to give Charlie a lift back to her flat, and when they arrived, proved a true gentleman by getting out of the cab, opening the door for her, and touching his forelock with a forefinger at her as they said their goodbyes.

"It's been a pleasure, ma'am," he told her with Old World American charm. "I'm flying back to the States tomorrow, but I'll be back shortly and I'd like to meet up again sometime."

Charlie left him and went into her apartment, where she mooned around quietly singing old Fred Astaire songs to herself.

She didn't think any more about Batty as she carried on her daily round, resting after her Broadway run, and so she was knocked out when, about a month and a half later, one of Batty's team rang and asked for her and her often stage partner Peter Mitchener to come for a screen test prior to casting for a film they were setting up of the old Songsters' hit *That Girl Next Door*.

The offer of film work appealed to Charlie. Apart from "recre-ating" an Astaire–Rogers style movie, she thought filming would be easier on her knee, which was not only aching quite a lot but would often swell up overnight.

The test took place in a barn of a building in South London and was Charlie's first real experience of film work. It only took one day, but she found it fascinating trying to keep a mood over several short "takes" that would be put together for a whole scene.

"I suppose you get used to the breaks. You suddenly stop in the middle of a dance while you lot move the cameras and lights and things," she said to a guy called Joe, the lighting cameraman.

"You should see us when we're working properly, for the real thing," replied Joe. "We're working twice as fast as usual today. We normally spend a lot more time making sure everything is as perfect as we can make it. But we've only got the studio for a day."

It was routine for the crew, but it was a complete novelty for Charlie, and she couldn't help giggling when, at the end, the direc-tor asked for close-ups of her full face and both profiles.

For some reason, Charlie didn't see the test. But then Batty rang her personally to tell her he wanted her to star in the film. He told her he'd had a script developed by an American writer, and—quite by chance, he said—it suited one of Hollywood's biggest names, Dane Winter, rather than Peter. Dane, an established film song-and-dance man with a jaunty on-screen manner and a cheeky grin, was interested, and terms were being lined up for him to star with her.

The news thrilled Charlie, but Peter was shattered that he had been overlooked—he had done really well in the test—and Charlie sympathised although she did not know what to say.

"I thought it was all set up for the pair of us," she told him.

Peter nodded dismally.

For a day or two, it was awkward between them, but then Peter got his good spirits back and for a while they started dating, going to see shows or films or simply going out for meals. Peter was always very proper in his behaviour towards Charlie, even when people stopped to ask for her autograph, or once even when a journalist came up to them in a restaurant and started asking questions about her relationship with Dane Winter.

"I haven't even met him," she replied truthfully, but the reporter was not satisfied and persisted with his questions.

In the weeks before detailed planning for the film got under way, Charlie and Peter, in fact, saw quite a lot of each other. Peter had started to fall for Charlie, but her feelings were purely friendly; there was no romance on her side at all.

Then Charlie got her script for the new screen role, and she began to get very busy as preparations built up towards the start of filming. She just didn't have much spare time, so the dating stopped.

The film was to be shot in England as it was cheaper and Charlie got off to a very bad start when she first went to the studio for dress fittings and meetings with make-up people and the like.

After lunching with the director, an old pro called Mackenzie Brownlow, it was suggested she go along to meet her co-star in his dressing room.

There was a long, single corridor connecting the various sound stages, with the dressing room blocks leading off between them, and Charlie waltzed down the corridor happily, turning into the dressing room block by pushing against the two-way swing doors. As she did so, Dane Winter came the other way, and the hard-thrust doors banged into his hands. Charlie thought she'd broken the American's wrist.

"What the...?" He stopped, seeing it was a girl. He switched. "Why don't you just watch where you're going?"

"I'm sor-sorry," stammered Charlie. "I was just on my way to see you."

"I don't like seeing anyone in my dressing room!" snapped the American.

Charlie apologised again, embarrassed, and told him who she was, and went pale as he snarled at her.

"Come back in half an hour then," he said curtly.

When she returned, Dane had recovered. His wrist was all right, and he flashed his well-known international smile at her.

"Sorry about that. Guess you really did catch me off my guard. My mind was on something else. I hope I didn't snap at you too hard," he said. "It's all OK now though. Wrist's fine. Episode forgotten."

Charlie was delighted. After that start, she was struck by the actual friendliness of her ruggedly handsome, experienced American co-star and they got on well.

"My real name is Michael Caine, but I couldn't really use that, could I? I've got the wrong accent," he told her on their first day working in the studio.

Dane was not all that tall—just a little taller than Charlie—but he looked much bigger than he was. He had friendly blue eyes, blonde wavy hair and smile creases at the side of his mouth. He was slim-hipped, but broad shouldered, and looked as a dancer should look.

Although their first few days together actually took place in a sound recording studio, they did spend half a day dancing off the cuff together to the music of the film to get to know each other as dancers and to "feel" the music. Each had an instinctive sense of the other's movements.

But the main part of the early days was spent rehearsing, then actually recording all the songs written originally for the stage show—but with two additional numbers especially for the film—onto a metallic disc. Dane had a powerful voice, and as with the dancing, from the beginning he and Charlie blended together harmoniously. The songs were good, the duets equally so, and both the stars managed well in their individual numbers. The technicians had very little to fix, so the track was completed within just a week and a day.

Then it was on to the actual sound stages for filming. Lights, cameras, microphones for the dialogue, dozens of technicians rushing around. It was all a strange, new and exciting world for Charlie.

Filming itself was different to anything she had known. Mackenzie, the director, had several good ideas, but he was rather fixed in his way and expected everyone else to know them. He did not allow for beginners and did not give a lot of advice to his actors, especially young and inexperienced people like Charlie. As a result, she soon began to lean on Dane for advice.

Filming was hard work, especially as she was not used to it, and she quickly found out that the "glamour" of film-making is a sham of a kind. Films, in themselves, are just make-believe, with audiences shown only what the director wants them to see to create a mood or tell part of his story, and Charlie soon discovered that the hard grind of repeating scenes, bits of scenes, close-ups, changes in dialogue, the vagaries of directors, producers, the other actors and sometimes the technicians was infuriating.

When filming the dance sequences, although she had thought it quaint during her test, she hated having to do just one step, one move, over and over with the cameras in different positions; performing a dance in bits did not allow her to get in the flow of it. In the theatre, she would have a partner who could react to, or even lead, an improvisation, but now she had to stick rigidly to the set routine—every time and every small bit.

"Can't we just do it?" she asked.

The cameraman tried using multi-camera set-ups in the shots, but they never seemed to give Mackenzie exactly what he wanted. So, it was repeat, repeat, repeat of the individual moves so the dance scenes could be built up.

It did not help when Mackenzie insisted she look at the small on-stage monitor after every shot to judge her own performance. Charlie could not relate to the small dancing figure on screen—it did not look like real dancing to her. She knew when something she had done was good or not; she did not need to see it.

At first she refused his insistence that she also go to the daily rushes to see the shot-by-shot record of the previous day's filming—she hated what she saw on a big screen even more than on the monitor—but after a while realised they were also necessary for continuity.

Apart from that, Charlie got used to film work. She still found it difficult in make-up and hairdressing. They were things she had always done for herself in the theatre, but here in a film studio everything had to match up exactly to scenes shot on previous days, so experts really were needed. Even between takes she had to endure the constant intrusion, or so it seemed to her, of the hair and make-up people.

It was a hard grind, especially for a beginner, and although she was quite a big name in theatrical terms, she was still a newcomer in a film studio and so she tended to hide in the background.

There were some lighter moments though. Charlie stifled a grin, for instance, when writers Harry and Danny came to visit the set one day, and before lunch, Danny was at the bar getting a round of drinks—soft for Charlie—when an aloof and recognisable Hollywood superstar tried to push in.

"Excuse me, I think I was first," said Danny.

"I don't do queues," she replied loftily. "I think you should just let me in first. Don't you know who I am?"

"Oh, are you famous then?" replied Danny straight-faced.

The actress was visibly annoyed, but stood back.

That amused Charlie, but she was not too amused when comedian Paolo Campello sat at the table with them after walking round behind their table and ostentatiously touching her shoulder. He gobbled his food, and was finished before both Charlie and Danny, then he belched silently, looked at his completely empty plate and said out loud, "I didn't like that one little bit."

He grinned at everyone, expecting laughs that didn't come.

"Can't really say I'm replete... but I'm certainly plete," he said.

He belched again quietly before Charlie and Danny stood to leave.

Another time, she and Dane were shooting a scene where he had to sing a romantic song to her, face to face and close up, and Charlie could not help giggling during the master shot as he mimed to the playback of his own voice. Although she eventually managed to control herself, it ruined several of the close-up shots too when she couldn't keep a straight face as she found herself just inches away from her miming co-star.

Charlie tried everything to learn the business from all angles, and spoke to as many people as she could, especially the so-called lesser members of the crew who always appreciated "one of the cattle" taking time for them. But apart from that, there was not only the inevitable boredom and waiting for the set-ups but the continual need to be nice, cheerful, and "on song" to people she didn't always like. She quickly learnt that a comedian has to be funny all the time, a lover romantic, a dancer lively and on her toes. They didn't always manage.

Paolo Campello—Paul Campbell in real life—for instance, had two sides to his real character. He could be very funny, with a seemingly natural and instinctive way of transposing the first letters of words in conversation: "What a girl" would come out as "Got a whirl" and the like.

But there was also a darker side to his real, take-home character. Once, waiting for a final lighting check, he was sitting on a chair when he called a young female assistant across to ask if he could have a mouthful of the water she was drinking.

"Just sippers?" he asked her, and the girl held out her glass.

With everyone watching, he cruelly made her put the glass on the floor. She did so, and Paolo looked at it for a moment.

"Not there. *There*," he said gruffly, indicating she should move it to his other side.

Blushing furiously, the girl did as she was told, then Paolo demanded she pick up the glass and hand it to him.

Paolo lifted the glass slowly to his lips, and drained it in one huge gulp, belching as he finished. He handed the empty glass back to the girl.

"Whoops, sorry. I know I said sippers. But I took gulpers by mistake," he leered.

Some of the crew laughed, embarrassed—it was typical Paolo—but the distressed girl simply took the empty glass and retreated to the back of the studio.

Paolo got his comeuppance on another day, however. He had been mugging up a comedy scene, frequently leading to the inevitable, "Cut it, let's go again." But after the fourth take, Marguerite Johnson, the film's second lead who was playing the scene opposite him as a friend of Charlie's character, snapped. They were filming on a raised dais, and Marguerite, an established romantic character actress more used to period dramas but in her first light-hearted "straight" part, stepped to one side, leant against the safety rail, and spoke softly and icily.

"Listen, you half-baked unfunny funny man," she exploded, "If you really want to know how to be funny, this is how you do it…"

For a full five minutes she explained the complicated techniques, the timing, the nuances, and all there was to know about playing a comedy role.

Everyone on set, including the director, stayed quiet and listened, although the monologue was all to Paolo Campello who had a world-wide reputation as a film comedian. When she had done, the crew applauded Marguerite and even Paulo had to admit she was right. He apologised both to her and to Mack when she was done.

But those were just incidents in the daily grind. Despite the boredom and her troubles having others do all the work she was used to, Charlie particularly loved the camera and sound crews, and found she could laugh and joke with them as well as the dressers who regularly fitted her with the required costumes, the make-up staff and the hairdressers.

She also got on well on personal terms with Marguerite. They usually ate together in the commissary, the mass catering restaurant used by the film crew and studio staff while stars and executives used the more exclusive dining room in the head office building, but one day they both joined Harry and Danny and producer Batty over lunch in the executive dining room.

They chatted about all sorts of things, until finally—casually—Danny asked Batty why he had chosen their escapist musical for filming. Batty smiled, reached into an inside pocket of his jacket, and pulled a small plastic card from his wallet. He told them he had had it printed when he was a young man as it summed up his feelings perfectly, and he had always carried it with him over the years to remind him of its values. It was a passage from Edna Ferber's successful novel, show and film *Show Boat*. He put his glasses on the end of his nose and read it to them.

The card quoted a passage from the book, and described how things often happen on stage that just do not happen in real life. Batty read it, then explained the effect it held for him.

"Audiences accept them. It's easy for them to understand," he said. "It's all there on a stage in front of them, and for a while they believe in the fantasy. It gives them a good feeling. The hero handsome, the heroine beautiful, and the villain is pure evil. Unlike real life, right always triumphs over wrong, and they can escape their own troubles. It's a magic world where they can laugh or sing—where they can escape realism."

Batty took off his glasses and put them down on the table next to the card. He looked round. "That's what movies are about. What show business is about," he said.

Charlie enjoyed that meal, but generally she preferred mixing with the crew. Dane too mingled easily with her and the crew. He had no airs or graces, and generally came over to everyone as Mr Nice Guy. He helped Charlie all he could. He was meticulous in rehearsal, although he had the experience to always make certain the camera majored on him.

But like Paolo Campello, he too had his "other" moments. About two weeks into shooting, he was in the sound recording studio early one morning as the crew prepared to shoot a number being sung by the second lead, Reggie Somers, who was playing Dane's character's closest friend. When the prerecorded playback music track was played for Reggie to mime to, he began singing in his own style, hitting different notes, breaking up lines, adding his own words. Director Mackenzie called a halt and began telling him off.

"Look, it's written one way and we can't have any ad-libbing," he told the actor. "You do it—"

"But I thought it improved things. We don't want lyrics like that," countered Reggie.

"What we don't want is you messing up the song. Just do it the way you're told."

"But—"

"No ifs or buts. Just do it the way I want it."

Reggie carried on and refused to stop arguing, so in the end it was finally decided to call in writers Danny and Harry to arbitrate. That meant a delay of a couple of non-productive hours, and immediately when they heard what was going on they insisted that Reggie stick to what was written: "Even if only as a matter of courtesy."

Reggie argued some more, and as by now it was early afternoon, with tempers frayed and, what Mackenzie called, "the artistic ethos" cool, it was decided to shut filming down for the day. As Mack retreated to the bar for a cooling-down drink with producer Batty, Dane followed him to the studio bar.

"I'm glad you didn't let Somers get away with that," he said, poking into the conversation. It's not the way we do things Stateside. There's no room for that kind of unprofessional behaviour in the business. I think you should take the song away from him to show who's boss."

Mack and Batty both nodded their heads, looking glum.

"Look," Dane continued, "If you want to keep the song in, I can do it."

The comment was added as if it was a complete afterthought and producer and director took it as an off the cuff idea and agreed, and as Dane left the bar, they immediately set about modifying the script. The next day, Reggie Somers was fired and a new second lead brought in—without a song to sing.

From the start, Batty had planned that Dane and Charlie would be billed as the new "Astaire–Rogers" in all publicity, and already had plans for a series of follow-up films featuring the couple. Once the first scenes of *That Girl Next Door* were shot and he saw the on-screen chemistry between them, he insisted that was the line to take.

Publicity man Phil Woodman and photographer Justin Makepeace, who had made his name as a royal "pictorial artiste", set up a photo session to get stills fostering the image, and on a rare day when neither was wanted on set, they turned up at Justin's West End gallery. To begin with, he just walked round taking pictures from a small hand-held mini camera, but then he said he wanted to set things up in a more stylised way.

As he was preparing things with a tripod and more formal lighting, he put on an old tape of Fred Astaire music and immediately Charlie began dancing round the studio to it. She was more relaxed than Dane, who—as always—was concerned over the image he gave out and took it all far more seriously. He kept telling her to slow down.

Charlie pressed him, and eventually made him stand up and join her. They went into one of their routines from the film.

Justin was delighted, and left his tripod and formal lighting to pick up an old 35 mm hand-held reflex camera to snap away as they danced.

"Great. Genius. Marvellous. Mag-nif-icent," he muttered over and over as he went through four complete rolls of film.

The pictures were good, and Phil Woodman had a great time showing them to Batty, Dane and Charlie. They planned to release one immediately, and the rest over the next several weeks. It was all part of a major publicity campaign built up to include DJs playing Fred Astaire discs of the time and getting stories in papers and magazines before the film's big West End preview.

Then Mackenzie finally called, "It's a wrap," at the end of the final shot, and filming was finished. Although Charlie had almost three more weeks of post-production work, she had time to relax. Her knee had given her a few small problems during the shoot but she had ignored it, but as she now took it easy, it again began to swell and hurt again. On her first day of non-filming freedom though, her former stage partner and romantic date Peter Mitchener called her fairly early in the morning to invite her out for dinner that evening. A delighted Charlie agreed.

Then Dane rang her at noon and he also asked her to join him for a meal that same evening. "Supper," he called it.

Once again Charlie agreed, and as soon as she put the phone down, she called Peter to postpone her date with him; Peter was very upset, but Charlie did not think too much about it.

For her, the film had turned out just like the old-fashioned Astaire–Rogers films she dreamt of, and in her romantic mind, the date with Dane was just an extension of that.

# Chapter 12

# THE ILLNESS

The "supper" with Dane was an excellent gourmet meal at a softly lit restaurant about an hour's drive from London, and Charlie enjoyed the whole evening. Dane was charming, funny, polite—he was the perfect, considerate host.

The meal was the first of many dates the couple had over the next month or so. They did a lot of things together. One day, they had fish and chips from paper bags soaked in vinegar. Charlie said she could not finish all hers, and Dane reached across and helped himself.

"You can always eat one more chip," he said as he over-stuffed several into his mouth, making her laugh.

Another time, he arranged to meet her early for a surprise outing. It turned out he had hired an extremely luxurious and expensive one-hundred-foot Azimut Leonardo cabin cruiser, complete with four crew for a week, and told her they were going for a "little jaunt" to the south of France. Immediately.

"I've got no clothes with me," said Charlie when he told her.

"Don't worry," replied Dane, "We can get you some when we get ashore."

Charlie found the boat, Princess C—"Especially chosen for you," he said—had eight berths.

"But there's just the two of us," said Dane.

They sailed before noon and put in again at the Port des Minimes in La Rochelle, a harbour along the French Atlantic coast. As they disembarked onto the Quai Marillac at around 6 p.m., Charlie looked at all the huge cabin cruisers docked nearby, dwarfing their boat, but she casually noted that Dane studiously ignored them.

Charlie loved the trip to the sunshine and getting away from the cold of England, although it was obvious that Dane was not keen on exposing himself to the elements and did not sunbathe very often. In La Rochelle, he waited for the sun to go down before going ashore, and she giggled to herself as she wondered whether it was just that he didn't want to ruin his perma-tan or just that he was scared no one in France would recognise him and ignore him. She banished the thought immediately.

That evening, they got a taxi and sat outside a small cafe fronting the Vieux Port sipping drinks, then wandered on to find a quiet restaurant on the rue St. Jean de Perot.

Although they were supposed to carry on down into the Mediterranean, Dane ordered his crew to sail home the next morning.

"Something's cropped up," he said.

Charlie couldn't help feeling he was a bit miffed because all the other boats in the marina seemed so much bigger than the one he had hired. Billionaires rather than millionaires. Again, she banished the thought quickly.

They left for home themselves by air after three days, and when they got there Dane was contrite. He realised how disappointed Charlie was that the trip had been cut short. To make up for it, the following day he booked her on the Eurostar to Paris, where he took her to the famous three-Michelin-starred Pierre Gagnaire restaurant, where he ostentatiously gave her a magnificent diamond bracelet.

"Dah-ling, it's magnificent, but so ex-pensive. You surely can't afford..." she began to joke in a theatrically regal voice before she realised he was being serious.

Although it annoyed him, Dane kept quiet.

Since the end of filming, Dane had changed. Charlie noticed he was more often bad tempered over small things—almost as if he didn't have a need to play the role of Mr Nice Guy without a big audience. He often showed small flashes of anger, much as he had done when Charlie had hit his wrists on that first day in the studio, but he usually managed to cover it up.

Charlie noted the change, but she never said a word about it. She thought she was falling in love yet again. In fact, she *had* fallen in love with the American, faults and all.

By now, Charlie had moved into a flat with Marguerite Johnson, who had played second lead in the film, although once again Dane didn't like it.

"You could have moved in with me," he said, eyebrows creased downwards.

"But, suh," replied Charlie with a mock Southern accent, "Ah'm a good girl."

They continued to date a lot, seeing each other every day. Then Charlie's producer and agent Aaron called her to say he'd been approached to see if she was ready to go back on stage—a new musical starring her with Dane. Without thought, and in a heady exhilaration, she told him to rush through and accept it.

That evening, Dane said he too wanted to do the show.

The new production was called *The Romance of Dance*, and everything about it was new for Charlie. For a start she did not have the support of Aaron as producer or Harry and Danny as writers and songsmiths, but she enjoyed the work, and being alongside Dane was a bonus. Rehearsals went very well, with the whole cast and crew friendly and happy, bookings high from the first announcement, and the show seeming to have the makings of yet another hit.

Her knee started swelling up again, but she ignored the pain and carried on. She told herself it was nothing more than overwork, and she ruggedly—and metaphorically—gritted her teeth and didn't let it worry her throughout rehearsals for the new show.

Opening night had been planned to fit in with the premiere of Charlie and Dane's film, which opened with glitzy West End razzamatazz: red carpets, cameramen, crowds, glamorous "celebrity" girls and handsome men. The reviews were way over the top. Everyone agreed it was a smash hit, and most critics readily picked up the Fred and Ginger publicity-fuelled angle for the two stars.

That carried over when the critics saw *The Romance of Dance*— once again they raved about Charlie and Dane, and the show was another instant hit. It settled into its long-run swing, and with Charlie and Dane being billed as—and quickly known as—"the new Fred and Ging", both the show and the film were proving to be smash hits. With a Hollywood follow-up offer for the current show in the wings, Dane proposed and Charlie happily accepted. Her world looked rosy. She was very much in love, and it showed in her work.

She seemed, however, to be putting too much into her dancing. Her legs started to give her trouble, and she began waking up during the night because of aches and pains, particularly in the left knee. The pains started slowly, and she again dismissed them as purely muscular caused by overwork.

Things went well until one Thursday matinee a couple of weeks later. Charlie and Dane both danced and sang well, but after the final curtain, Charlie had to turn down Dane's offer to go for a long lunch before the evening performance.

"I'm feeling so tired," she said. "I ache all over, and all I want to do is sleep. You go. Let me rest."

Dane protested, but she eventually persuaded him and he went off.

Charlie slept for a couple of hours during the rest of the afternoon, and woke refreshed well before it was time to get ready for the evening curtain up. There was something in the air that Thursday evening. More than normal, Charlie sensed the packed audience building up on the other side of the curtain, waiting with anticipation, and she was eager to get the show under way. It was a very special feeling, and that night she danced superbly—leaps, pirouettes, spins even better than usual. The rest of the cast picked up her mood and played to her, and even Dane was prepared to take a bit of a back seat and let her have the glory. And after one solo routine, he joined in and clapped as she got a round of applause from the cast and crew backstage as well as a standing ovation from the audience.

At the end of the show, there were no less than fifteen curtain calls. Dane, as co-star, stepped forwards with Charlie at the end of the first four of those, then the audience started chanting, "Charlie, Charlie, Charlie, Char-lee," and he joined the rest of the cast standing back to let her take centre stage for the rest. Charlie felt like she was floating; she had never felt like that before.

She went to bed thoroughly exhausted and fell into a deep, deep sleep. But next morning, she was particularly achy. Her legs still hurt, her feet felt on fire, her left knee was swollen. By the evening, she could barely walk, but she began to feel a little better before curtain up and was able to start the show. After the first act though, she had to call it a day. She could barely stand. Her understudy took over.

Her legs, feet and left knee were still inflamed the next morning, and Charlie could not appear in either of Saturday's two shows, although after staying in bed and resting for the whole weekend she felt better and was back on stage on the Monday. But at the end of the evening performance, she was once again suffering. And the pain was so intense that she woke several times that night unable to get rid of the violent ache in her knee.

The show physio worked on her over the next few days, and Charlie was able to perform, but not at the level she was used to or wanted. She was unsatisfied that she was moving freely enough, and Dane too said he felt she was somehow holding back. In one show, some of the girls threw in a few extra little bits to cover her when it seemed she was pausing to rest her leg, but Charlie dismissed the fact that she was frequently waking at night with pains, particularly in her knee. She did not want to accept that there could be anything wrong.

As the pain grew and began to get even more frequent, however, she was eventually forced to go see her doctor. She told him she felt it was just that she had been overworking—putting too much stress on her knees while dancing night after night for such a long time without rest. He examined her, and immediately decided to send her for X-rays and a blood test, and then on to a specialist consultant. He was concerned.

# BIG C

The surgery was at the far end of a large health centre, and Charlie made her way slowly towards it unaware that people recognised her and watched her limping. The outer office of the surgery was full—people of all ages, with young children running around and all the adults looking a little worse for wear. She gave her name to the receptionist, and sat waiting to be called by the electronic board high on one side.

When her name did eventually appear, she limped to Surgery 4, where consultant Mr Charles Robertson sat in front of a large desk rather than in the deep swivel chair behind it.

"I won't ask how you are. I'm supposed to tell you," he said with a professional smile and a twinkle in his eye.

But when Charlie told him, the humour disappeared.

"How long have you had this pain?" he asked her.

Charlie explained that she had ached more than usual for some time—probably over a year—and said she hadn't taken too much notice of the pain, because she felt it was part of being a dancer. But, she stressed, it had been getting much worse lately, and it had meant she had been unable to perform on a couple of occasions.

The doctor gravely made notes, then asked exactly where the pain was.

Charlie pointed to her left knee, and as he bent forwards to examine it, he bit his lower lip.

"I've seen your X-rays, but I wonder, did you have a fall? Or bang it in any way?" he finally asked.

"Well..." Charlie paused and thought, "I did get a bit of a kick on the shin some months back. But that's usual. The physio looked at it and gave me some heat treatment, and it seemed to go away. I didn't think any more about it. It happens all the time when you're dancing. But it's come back, and one evening, my leg just gave way and the pain has been getting worse ever since."

It was a bit of a muddled explanation, and the consultant looked concerned in a doctorish way. He pursed his lips.

"Is there any... any medical history in your family?" he eventually asked.

"No, nothing I can think of."

"Nothing at all like this?

"No. At least, I don't think so. Is it important?"

The doctor shook his head, but he was perturbed. He took Charlie's symptoms seriously—apart from the X-rays, other tests had given him a good idea as to what the problem was and he had more than a sneaking feeling it was a malignant growth. He didn't tell her.

"There's a little lump showing there, but that could be caused by any one of several things," he told her. "Any pain like this should be checked, and I'm going to send you for a second opinion and ask for some more tests. I don't think there's anything for you to worry about, but I do want to be sure."

Mr Robertson walked round the desk and sat in the swivel chair. He asked if Charlie wanted a private clinic, but when she said she didn't think anyone should have preferential treatment, he assured her that the local NHS hospital would be the best.

"The people I know there are the same ones who do the private work at the Claymore Clinic. You know, the one that rhymes with 'pay more'!"

He smiled at the regular joke, making some notes on a pad in front of him. "You'll get just as good treatment there, probably better. Leave it with me. I'll fix the appointment and they'll be in touch. They'll explain all the tests."

Charlie went back to the show and tried to carry on dancing, but the knee was troubling her more and more. Dane, her co-star as well as her fiancé, would cover for her sometimes, but he always complained afterwards that he was carrying her through the show.

"I can't help it. It's not my fault," she told him.

"Then whose fault is it?" he would reply gruffly.

Charlie had to bite back the angry reply that instantly came to mind, and later assured herself that Dane's bad moods were brought on because of his anxiety about her injury.

Dane seemed considerate to start with, but as Charlie began missing days at the theatre—which annoyed her as much as him—he began to get more irritable.

"Can't you take a painkiller?" he asked.

Charlie had tried that, but she didn't say anything.

On other days, he asked why she didn't just grit her teeth and dance on. "That's what a true pro would do," he said unfeeling.

Charlie was upset by Dane's growing grumbles, but she normally held back any comment. Then one day, the day on which she received the letter calling her for her hospital appointment, they had a terrific row after she had asked in a cold voice why he didn't just support her instead of complaining.

"I can't stand the tumble of being associated with a cripple and someone who's heading to be a nobody who never turns up for shows," he said cruelly. "It's *my* reputation on the line."

Charlie burst into tears and, before the show that evening, asked the show physio to look at her knee yet again, asking if there was anything he could do to see her through. He offered, and gave her heat treatment, but just before the big finale, her leg gave way and she fell to the stage. She somehow managed to make it look as if she meant it—like the dying swan—but as Dane danced on, two of the girls covered for her and the audience did not seem to notice.

The pain was increasing, and with the missing performances beginning to mount up, Charlie reluctantly pulled out of the show. The next morning, Dane sent her a twelve-word note saying it would be best for all concerned if they broke off the engagement. His reaction hurt Charlie and, once again, she felt just like the shy little girl she had been before she found she could dance.

She tried to ring Dane, but only got an impersonal answering service—not even in his own voice—and she left a message. He did not return the call, and in the following days Charlie tried to ring several more times, but before anything could happen, events began to take over. She was either too involved in medical matters or too ill to chase Dane.

The day of her hospital appointment arrived, and she went to see another specialist consultant, Mr Bernard Wyatt. The name on the door said he was an oncologist, but that didn't mean a thing to Charlie. Mr Wyatt gave her knee a lengthy examination before telling her that, because he could feel a slight lump just below it, he wanted to scan it to see if there was any abnormal or diseased tissue.

He said he could fix it for the following day, but told Charlie that taking the scan itself would be a long and tiresome process. She would have to come in for an injection, and it would then take another two or three hours before that would have any effect and so allow for the actual scan.

Charlie went away slightly baffled, but feeling she was in safe hands. Mr Wyatt had shown a quiet, reassuring manner that put her at her ease.

As a result, when she arrived at his surgery the next day, she was in quite a good mood. As advised, she wore a loose blouse and skirt, and she chatted easily to a pretty nurse who took her into a small cubicle and asked her to roll up one of her sleeves.

"I'm just going to inject a little bit of what we call a radiophar-maceutical," she explained. "People call it a dye because it shows up when we scan you, but it isn't a dye. It's a radioactive drug." She had a twinkle in her eye because she knew the reaction the word would get.

She laughed as she saw the predictable look on Charlie's face. "Oh no, we're not going to blow you up. It's only a small dose, and it's quite harmless."

The nurse handled the blue-coloured injection professionally, and when it was over, she told Charlie to rest before the actual scan roughly two hours later. Charlie was taken to a small, airy side ward where she lay on a bed while the drug worked its way round her body. She didn't feel anything, and the nurse reappeared at various stages to monitor her before a little over two hours later she was taken in for the scan itself.

Mr Wyatt was there this time and after greeting her jovially, he retreated to another room screened off from her and worked with an operator as the knee was scanned. It seemed a long process to Charlie, and took almost an hour.

Then when it was over, Mr Wyatt said the scan had showed a small, unusual dark mass, a "hot spot", which had to be investigated because it worried him. He said he would like to make a further series of examinations as a result, and Charlie was taken back to her bed, where she expected him to take the extra tests. But the nurse brought her a weak, sugary cup of tea and told her to relax.

"You can go home when you feel right," she said, explaining that the other tests needed to be set up. "Don't worry, it's just that Mr W seems intrigued by today's scan. From my point of view, I don't think I've ever seen anything like this before."

Charlie didn't know what to make of that, but she went home and prepared to wait for a long time. It was only four more days before she heard from the surgery though—a letter in which Mr Wyatt said he would like her to have an MRI, a magnetic resonance imaging scan, which would highlight the area around the dark spots the bone scan had showed.

Once again, there was a short delay and the MRI didn't take place for another three weeks.

Charlie's knee was painful all the time now, and with the worry about what the first scan might have shown, she was in a bit of a fright when she turned up for the next session.

The young operator who greeted her quickly put her at ease and explained the procedure in simple words. The scan, he said, comprised taking imaging X-rays to see, first of all, if the problem around her knee had shown signs of metastasis—spreading—and to see if there was any evidence of bone destruction. Along with her previous tests, they would help confirm a definite diagnosis.

The scan, he explained sympathetically, was not like quite an X-ray. Instead, it used magnetic fields to produce detailed pictures of her body. He said she would be given another injection—a special contrast dye to make her "inside bits" easier to see.

Charlie had to fill in a standard form about her previous health and medical history—there was little she could write down there— then she signed a form consenting to the scan. She was asked to remove her watch, earrings and a necklace, which the operator stored in a locker, saying he was pleased that she had acted on the advice in her notification letter and had worn a dress without zips or buttons and with a tie-up sash rather than a buckled belt.

"You'd be surprised at how many people ignore what they're told and have to strip almost right down!" he laughed.

Then he gave Charlie the injection of the contrast dye, which luckily had no effect on her, and took her to the scan room.

Inside was a large, slightly off-white machine, a short open-ended cylinder with a flat bed protruding at one end. It was, said the operator, a special magnetic resonance imaging machine which used a powerful magnet linked to a computer to create even more detailed pictures of areas inside the body,

Charlie was asked to lay full length on the bed with her skirt pulled up as high as she could get it.

"It's lucky I'm wearing clean knickers," she joked.

The operator laughed again as he put a small frame over her knees and told her to relax, although she seemed quite at ease.

He then went into another room behind a huge glass window which allowed him to see the machine and allowed him to talk to Charlie through a monitor.

When all was ready, he told Charlie to keep as still as she could, and then the motorised bed took her feet first into a huge doughnut-shaped revolving disc inside the machine that moved along the length of her left leg around the knee, taking a series of detailed internal pictures from different angles. These would allow the experts to create a complete computer image of the area.

At first, Charlie expected to feel claustrophobic inside the machine, but her fears soon subsided and she relaxed almost to the point of falling asleep. The machine made some loud tapping noises occasionally as the scanned coils were switched on and off, and the operator—Charlie wished she knew his name as she lay still inside the cylinder—spoke constantly, giving soothing advice as he took the pictures.

The scans only lasted a few seconds each, and finally after some twenty minutes the bed slid easily out of the scanner.

A few minutes later, the operator returned to the scan room and helped Charlie onto her feet. She felt a little tottery at first, but recovered quickly as he took her back to the reception room and sat with her over the inevitable cup of tea while he filled in a few forms.

When they had finished drinking, he told Charlie it was all over. She could go home and carry on as normal. She walked out to the street still wondering what his name was.

After that, it was just a case of waiting again. She thought that when it was all over, she would only be given some medicine or something before she returned to work, to dancing.

It seemed an age before all the results were in and Charlie was back in Mr Wyatt's office. He had a folder with a lot of photographs inside—X-ray and MRI photographs—and he studied them for a few moments before he spoke.

The silence seemed to affect Charlie.

"I've had more pictures taken of the inside of my leg than I ever had stills when I was trying to get agents and producers interested in me," she told Mr Wyatt to fill the silence. She was joking, but it was only to cover the uneasiness she felt.

"Well, we just want to check exactly what's going on inside," he replied cheerfully. He was always cheerful with the patients. "There's no need to worry. It looks like there might be a small growth there, but I wouldn't think it's any threat to life." He almost chuckled as he spoke, but Charlie didn't see the funny side.

The consultant was matter-of-fact, but he was, in fact, worried. With the results of all the tests in, he said he now wanted to take a biopsy, explaining that it meant inserting a needle-like instrument into the back of the knee to take a small sample of the growth "and anything nasty round it". Once again, he told Charlie not to worry about it.

Charlie did worry a bit because there was an eleven-day wait before she could be taken in to the clinic for the procedure. A junior doctor, Mark McGhee, carried it out, asking Charlie to once more sign a conssent form before getting her to sit on the side of a bed covered with a blue sheet of paper and giving her a local anaesthetic to numb the whole area around her knee.

Once the knee was "dead", Dr McGhee carefully inserted the thin hollow biopsy needle in the back of her knee. Charlie could feel it poking round, but felt no pain. As he probed, the doctor explained that apart from the lump that appeared to be there and which he found without problem, he would also take what he called "a bone marrow aspiration"—getting a sample of the fluid around the area.

Charlie was surprised she understood what he was talking about—she was getting used to the mass of technical terms used by all the medical teams.

The biopsy didn't take long, and after giving time for the effects of the anaesthetic to wear away, Charlie was allowed home, where she once again had to wait for the results. It seemed to her that lots of things were happening with no end result, but she managed to convince herself that it was better to wait and get things right.

The initial result didn't take all that long. It was just three days before she was once more called in to see Mr Wyatt. He told her that the biopsy had been positive and had shown that there was definitely a polyp—that didn't mean anything to Charlie—although the pathologist who'd analysed it was still not sure if it was malignant or not.

Waiting was a painstaking business, and it took a further ten days to check. While waiting, Charlie went to visit a rehearsal of "her" show. Dane was not there and neither she nor any of the others mentioned his name. Charlie felt remote from it all and left after about half an hour with everyone, including herself, vowing to keep in touch.

Then after two and a bit weeks, Mr Wyatt called her in, and in rather technical terms told her the biopsy showed that she appeared to have, what he called, an osteogenic sarcoma, which he described as an aggressive growth inside a bone. In her case, it had started at the top of the tibia, the longer leg bone, and had spread round to the knee cap which joins onto it.

There was now a sizeable growth in an area behind her left knee which had started growing through the bone wall and was spreading into her calf and thigh. Mr Wyatt said it would need surgery to get rid of it before it grew even bigger.

The news was obviously a shock to Charlie. She didn't like the sound of it at all, and although a number of questions instantly sprang to her mind, she couldn't think of a thing to say.

Mr Wyatt was sympathetic, and calmly went on to tell her what he planned to do to rid her of the problem. He would arrange for a colleague, Colin Edwards, to carry out the actual surgery, and in the meantime would have more blood tests taken to check her kidneys and liver, and get X-rays of her lungs.

Mr Wyatt sent her off to have the tests, and when they were done Charlie saw him again.

"All's well," he told her. "But we had to check. The biggest fear with osteosarcoma is that the cancer has spread to the lungs. That's the next place it usually goes. In your case, it hasn't, luckily,"

The C word was out and Charlie heard it, although she could not connect with it. Cancer was something that happened to old people, poorly people. But not young, fit dancers.

"I didn't even know you could get cancer in the bone," she told Mr Wyatt.

"I'm afraid so," the consultant said rather sadly. "But don't worry, there's at least an eighty-five percent recovery rate. You'll be fine." He was calm and collected, matter-of-fact and encouraging.

Mr Wyatt assured Charlie that the treatment was not as dire as in the old days, when it was a certainty that an osteosarcoma would mean having the leg amputated.

"We rarely have to do that nowadays," he said.

Charlie was shocked again. She had not anticipated that. She had thought pills or injections might work.

"An operation? Will that affect my dancing?" she asked.

Mr Wyatt tilted his head sideways and raised his eyebrows, but he did not say anything.

He indicated that the consultation was over, and as Charlie stood to leave, he picked up the next file and opened it.

"Mrs O'Connell," he muttered quietly. "Oh yes, she's the old biddy who always complains about her legs."

He sighed and, as Charlie left the room, a middle-aged lady passed her going in to take her place. As she held the door open to let the other woman pass, Charlie looked back over her shoulder saw that Mr Wyatt had switched on his smile and stood expansively.

"Edith," he said genially. "Great to see you again. You're looking well. Here, have a seat and we'll talk about things..."

Charlie gave herself an inward wry grin. The charm had been a professional air—good at the time but meaningless. She was just another patient.

The next step was for Charlie to meet the younger consultant, Colin Edwards, who had been recommended by Mr Wyatt as the best man to carry out the operation.

It was six days before that happened, and in a subconscious effort to keep from thinking about her big C and its possible effects on her future, Charlie began to wonder what Dane was up to. It was just an occasional thought that came to her as she was resting, and it only affected her once—when she began to get angry at his apparent indifference. But the anger soon passed as she went to meet Mr Edwards.

He was a jolly, friendly man with twinkling eyes who looked nowhere near his fifty-seven years. "Hello, I'm the man who's going to get you better," he said. "What do I call you?"

"Charlie."

"And I'm Colin. Don't let the hospital sisters bully you into calling me anything else. They tend to be a bit formal."

On the wards later, Charlie could see that all the nurses and junior doctors adored him, and from the moment she met him, she did too.

There was no nonsense from Mr Edwards. After a few immediate preliminary niceties, he got down to business straightaway and suggested a short course of what he called preliminary neo-adjuvant, pre-operation chemotherapy to try to reduce the size of the growth.

"Chemo is supposed to kill off the bad cells, and that will hopefully make it easier for me to remove the tumour before I try to cut out the bit of bone with the growth and replace it with a light metal rod," he told her.

Charlie's brow furrowed.

"Provided no cancer cells are found at the edge or border of the tissue removed during surgery, we can minimise the amount of healthy tissue removed with it. Then after that, well, there'll be another final palliative session of chemo as a preventative measure to make sure there are no malignant cells left, either in the same part of the leg or in other parts in the body."

Charlie was baffled by it all. Chemotherapy and metal rods? Nobody had mentioned that before.

"It all makes it sound serious," she said.

Mr Edwards gave her a reassuring smile. "Yes, it is serious," he replied, "But don't worry. It's nowhere near as bad as it sounds."

He told here that, although he couldn't give a definite timeline, he reckoned it could take an initial two and a half months of chemo to shrink the tumour, then about a month to get over it and have the surgery, and finally a further two and a half months or so of more chemo to take the total treatment time to around six months.

"In my opinion, although it's a long time it has to be done," he added.

Despite all that, Charlie knew she had to put her life in Mr Edwards' hands and signed all the consent forms for the treatment and operation on the spot. She felt she should have been distraught or something, but although she was apprehensive, she was really quite calm and matter-of-fact about it.

The whole process though had seemed to take a long time for just a pain in a knee.

# Chapter 14

# CHEMO

It was not long before Charlie was called in to the Mercury Ward of St. Mary's General Hospital, where she was met by a chemotherapy specialist, Dr Charles Hacker, and from the start she found him incredibly remote and apparently unconcerned for individuals. She presumed he was just too hard worked.

In the days before the appointment date was posted to her, Charlie had begun worrying. From the outset the whole idea of chemotherapy was a bit of a worry. Chemo? Well, that was big time. Big. *Big* time. However, she had been told it would be wise to undergo it, and she had agreed without too much concern.

Now it was with her.

Her first visit lasted about twenty minutes though, and had nothing to do with actual treatment. Hacker told her she would have a preliminary round of eight sessions to try to shrink the tumour, and after the operation, a further six as a precautionary measure to ensure the malignancy had not spread. He spoke of what was going to happen during the treatment, and warned Charlie that the drugs she would be given did not differentiate between cancerous and normal cells.

"That means they can produce various side effects such as a numbness in the fingers and toes, irritable skin, nausea, possibly diarrhoea, a difficulty in swallowing, and mouth sores. And you'll likely get a nasty taste in your mouth," he said calmly, reciting the symptoms as if he was reading from a list. "You may get all of them, or just one, or maybe none. But you should know they are a possibility.

"I have to tell you too that there's a good chance your hair will fall out, although it should grow again after the treatment is finished, albeit possibly in a different colour." He paused. "Oh yes, and there's also a distinct possibility that it will affect your future fertility."

He smiled reassurance, but although Charlie thought momentarily of Dane, she was quite impervious to that idea.

As Dr Hacker finished speaking, an elderly nurse who had been sitting listening quietly in a corner of the consulting room stood up.

"Miss Whittaker," she began, "We're conducting a series of tests with some new drugs that have been in use for some time in America but are new to England. Although it will extend the time of your treatment, we'd like you to think about joining in the experiments..."

Charlie shook her head vigorously. "No. No, I don't want to do that," she replied.

"Well, perhaps you could think about it and let us know when you next come in."

Charlie shook her head again. She didn't want to think about it. Events were suddenly moving far too quickly for her to think about experiments. Or even to be scared. Seeing that the nurse was likely to argue, Hacker took over once more to talk of the treatment Charlie would be receiving, explaining that his team had decided that her "combination chemotherapy" would be a cocktail of three drugs that kill rapidly dividing cells. He did not explain what any of these drugs were for or did.

Finally, he gave Charlie one more choice. He said she would have to have a catheter inserted to receive the drugs, and he asked where she wanted it to go. He told her the PICC—a peripherally inserted central catheter—was a long, thin, flexible tube which had to be inserted into one of her veins and slid through the inside of it until it reached an even larger vein. At the end of the tube outside the body, there would be a special closed cap that could be opened to attach a drip or syringe through which the drugs would pass. It would be left in for the entire duration of the chemo treatment.

Charlie had the choice—it could be inserted either in the crook of her right elbow or in her right shoulder. If in the elbow, the line would run up the vein to her shoulder, take a sharp turn and go across to link up with the main vein somewhere just above the heart. He said the shoulder line would be shorter, but would need to be inserted under some kind of anaesthetic by a doctor. Charlie chose the elbow.

With that, it was indicated that the consultation was at an end. As Charlie left the room, the nurse—who had been trying to "sell" her on the experiment and had accompanied the final minutes of the discussion with a few silent snorts—glared at her.

A week later, Charlie attended her first working session at the clinic.

The ward was shaped like a square letter J—a long, tall, neutral painted room connected by a short corridor filled with equipment to a parallel smaller room. Chairs of all shapes and sizes were placed in both the legs of the ward, and people were sitting with metal stands holding plastic tubes dangling into their arms or shoulders. None of them looked up as Charlie walked in.

The lead nurse in the chemo ward, Chris—Charlie never did find out his surname—was tall and angular, with a ready smile and a willing helpfulness. He was one of no more than seven or eight nurses working the ward flat out in long shifts. They dealt with upwards of four hundred patients in every five-day week.

He greeted her cheerfully when she arrived for her first chemo session, and strapped a plastic bracelet with her name, date of birth and hospital number on her left wrist and told her she had to wear it until the treatment was over. Blood pressure, pulse, temperature and urine were checked, and she was given a test to check blood count and kidney function. Chris told her the first thing was to have the PICC line inserted on the inside of her right arm.

"It's called a Hickman line, by the way, but you needn't worry about that. It's just our posh name for it," he said. "You have to have a posh name in the NHS or the suits won't know what to order or talk about over their G & Ts."

Like most newcomers to the chemo ward Charlie had been worried when she was originally told about the line—now she was not quite terrified, but terribly apprehensive that it was going to be fed inside her. In the event, it couldn't have been easier.

One of the specialist nurses came to her bedside, drew the curtain round it, and reassured her. The Indonesian nurse, whose name tag told that she was called Widya, cleaned both Charlie's arms with a damp piece of cloth, then rubbed some sort of jelly-like anaesthetic onto the inside of both her elbows—although they were aiming for the right one, they numbed both down in case they couldn't find a suitable vein—and told her to wait while the stuff "took". As Widya went away, she pulled the curtain open so Charlie could see round the ward.

It took almost an hour during which Charlie just sat on the bed blankly, then Widya returned with an assistant, both dressed in operating theatre blue and with face masks and rubber gloves. They closed the curtains again, and Charlie was asked to lie on the bed on her left side with her right arm extended behind her, and then told she would feel a slight pinprick as if having an injection. She barely felt a thing, and before she realised it, in a matter of minutes she was told to turn onto her back.

"How's it going?" she asked.

"Done," said Widya, all friendly smiles.

The line was taped into the crook of her elbow—and through it into the vein—with the outer section taken down from there to connect to a small cap called a lumen taped into position inside her lower forearm a few inches above the wrist, to which the plastic bags of drugs would be attached.

The whole insertion process had taken less than ten minutes, then Widya called a volunteer helper across to take Charlie down to an X-ray room two floors below, where from behind a glass barrier she actually saw a screen showing the line in place inside her. As she had been told, it went up her arm, turned at the shoulder, then went across inside her chest and down to the vein near her heart.

But it was not in the right position!

Charlie was taken back upstairs to the ward, where the whole process was carried out again and this time the X-ray showed the line accurately positioned.

Charlie was told to sit for a few minutes before being told she could go home to let the line settle in overnight. No problems. Why had she been uneasy about it?

During that evening, Charlie only occasionally realised she had the line strapped to her right forearm, but it did not unduly worry her.

Then, as instructed, she reported back to the ward the next day, where Chris offered her a seat in a battered old armchair and brought across an upright metal stand with two plastic bottles hanging from two hooks at the top. He fixed tubes from the bottles into the lumen attached to the cannula line on her arm, and the chemo drugs and a saline drip began dripping into her system. A monitoring machine was attached and placed in front of her giving various readings, and with a clock counting down the time of the drips.

Others in the ward ignored all that was going on. Some were reading books, one had earphones on and was listening to music, most just sat and looked into space. No one spoke.

Charlie couldn't feel anything as she sat for two hours counting down the time until all the drugs were in, dripping two drops at a time. It was slow, but the two hours soon passed and when the bottles were empty, they replaced the drip line with an infuser to add more of the drugs through a plastic bottle she had to wear overnight. Charlie had been told it would be about the size of a mobile phone that she could strap to her waist. It turned out to be like an old-fashioned half-pint milk bottle, weighing as much and a bit bulky. It was strapped to her belt, and she soon got used to it.

A taxi had been booked beforehand, and it was waiting as Charlie left the centre in a steady downpour of freezing rain and high winds. Charlie huddled into her dark blue raincoat, with a scarf wrapped round her mouth to save breathing in the cold air and her hands thrust deep into her pockets to keep them warm.

She found the taxi and went to the passenger door, automatically grabbing the handle. It was freezing, and she got an instant electric tingle in her fingertips—something she had been warned about. Luckily, once inside the cab, she warmed up and the feeling quickly wore off.

Well, she thought it had. Later that evening, she took a bottle of milk from the fridge and the tingle came back. *Lesson one*, she thought, *always wear gloves or use a rag to get cold things from cold places*.

The next day, Charlie went to see a district nurse in her GP's clinic at the health centre to have the infuser removed and the line washed through—this time with a syringe attached to the lumen—

and a week later she returned to the hospital oncology ward as arranged. But the visit began badly. The taxi was late, and Charlie barely had enough time to report in and literally had to run to the outpatients reception despite the pain in her knee.

Puffing, blowing and feeling very unfit—well, she was supposed to be ill—she faced up to a po-faced receptionist.

"Have you had your blood test?" asked the stern-faced lady behind the counter.

"Several," she replied.

The receptionist glared. "Since the first session!!!" There were definitely three exclamation marks.

"No."

"You have to have one before seeing the doctor!!!" said the reception dragon. She gave Charlie another three exclamation marks, then told her to go to the outpatients waiting area.

Charlie did so and waited alongside dozens of other patients sitting with glazed eyes like turned-off headlamps.

She was there for almost two hours, and although she queried it once, as did most of the others, she was told she was in the queue and that there was only one doctor, although she had frequently seen at least two or more people in an office at the side looking like doctors with stethoscopes worn casually around their necks.

Finally, she was called in to an inner sanctum examination room, and there she waited some more. This time it was only for ten minutes before what seemed like a twelve-year-old Polish lass with the title "Doctor" on her name tag—she was not one of those seen chattering earlier—came in and told her the delay was because her notes had been sent to the wrong consultant's clinic.

This time there were three silent exclamation marks from Charlie for the receptionist who had despatched her.

After that, the young doctor gave her a thorough examination which lasted all of three minutes, then asked where her case notes were. Charlie told her she had no idea—there were a few Polish exclamation marks from the doctor this time—and she was told they had to be found immediately as it was vital before the next session of chemo could be arranged for the following week. It was necessary to check that her white cells were building up to the required strength to fight the chemo drugs.

"I thought that was why I was here. To have a blood test," said Charlie.

"Wait outside," ordered the doctor.

Charlie went out and waited some more.

After twenty minutes or so, a nurse brought out the requisite blood test form—well, two actually, as she had preplanned the next visit in two weeks—and Charlie dutifully wandered off to the test unit. The staff there had, by this time gone to lunch, and instead Charlie was directed to the main hospital test unit to join a queue, and a further twenty-five minutes on, it was all done—cheerfully and painlessly.

Charlie staggered back to the outpatients, and finally got the all-clear for the following week's session. She staggered off and went home.

An hour or so later, the phone rang.

"It's the clinic here. Did you go for the blood test?" asked a voice.

The following week, it was back to the Mercury Ward. The irritation of the previous visit to the hospital had faded as Charlie realised how hard all the staff in the oncology hospital had to work: too many patients, too few nurses, too demanding consultants.

As she reported in for the second session, Charlie was greeted by head nurse Chris and quickly put back on the drip for another two hours, the infuser bottle was replaced, and she was sent smiling into the afternoon after a fine, free, three-course hospital lunch in which the thick chicken soup and crème brûlée pudding were particularly delicious. It was all so matter-of-fact.

But although the second session was pretty much as the first, this time the people were different. An elderly woman sitting next to her smiled sympathetically.

"You're new here, aren't you?" asked the older women, introducing herself as Jane.

Charlie nodded.

"I'm an old hand," said Jane. "I've had eight sessions. It seems a long time, but it soon goes."

They started to chat—generalities, nothing special considering the importance of the circumstances of their being together—and eventually, encouraged by Charlie and Chris, quite a few of the others joined in. It was the start of what Charlie came to call the Chemo Club: a happyish bunch of drip-feeders and infuser-carriers who were all members of a club that no one really wanted to join.

Most of the patients were women. The majority on drips like Charlie, although there was one lady stretched out on a bed for some reason. An elderly man grumbled a little, but on the other hand another woman said she had not suffered any side effects at all from the treatment. Charlie quickly heard that most of them had suffered, but she was determined to try to ignore everyone's advice and to wait and see how it affected her.

"The nurses are all so good. They won't let you suffer," said Jane.

Charlie knew people were only trying to be helpful, but she wasn't going to let other people's experiences, which all seemed so different, affect her.

Luckily, after that second session, she felt no real side effects apart from tingling fingers and a vague soreness at the back of her throat, and she went away happy. Things seemed to be OK. Chemo, she began to think, was easy.

It was, she realised, a necessary ordeal, but chemotherapy was a frightening word. It was the big one and meant something quite terrifying really. Eventually though, going to Chemo Club meetings just became a habit she had to endure, and although she found Mercury a wonderful ward with more than wonderful nurses running it, it was time-consuming and uncomfortable, and somewhere she didn't really want to be.

The third session went as before, but as soon as it was over Charlie began to feel extremely ill. She was not able to walk, she felt nauseous, and the nurses had to get a wheelchair to take her to her taxi afterwards. But the feeling passed after a night's sleep.

# Chapter 15

# MORE CHEMO

Charlie was feeling very lonely. She was missing the comradeship of the show, missing the overall excitement of the theatre. And hanging over her there was still the unpleasantness of the next spell of chemo that was to come.

Although there were only a couple of weeks between sessions, in some ways she strangely also missed the comradeship of the Chemo Club: nurses and patients.

As she waited for the next call, she was surprised at people's reactions to her. She seemed ignored when she went into the streets—or so she thought—but after a while it hit her that there was no reason for people to know her now. She realised that she was only looking at her past—a past that now seemed a long way away.

Charlie made herself think of the present, of her current position. She missed dancing tremendously, and she often thought of possibly having to give it up—albeit temporarily, she still hoped—and she missed the delight of performing to music. She missed the sheer glamour and fizz of curtain up. It was better than being ill, she reasoned, but she still had an ache for her life on stage.

She felt very insignificant and alone.

Fortunately, the next dose of chemo, the fourth, wasn't bad. Charlie was prepared for the nausea and forced herself to bite back the bile as she was having the infusions. However, it was at the end of that week that a whole pile of new side effects kicked in. Apart from the usual two days of tingling fingertips and the ache in the jaw with the first mouthful of food on the first day or so after the chemo, all the things she had been warned about happened in small doses.

She had a lot of indigestion, irregular bowels, lots of wees especially overnight, a lot of wind, a dry metallic taste in her mouth—although a more than healthy appetite—a slight dizziness on a couple of occasions, and a throaty feeling for two days.

But they all passed, and as the next visit to the clinic was to show, it was all part of the scheme of things. This time there was a comparatively short wait at the start of her next visit to the clinic, just an hour and forty minutes in the outpatients reception, before being called in to the examination room. She was weighed, then waited there alone for about fifteen minutes before opening the door so she could chat to the patients still waiting outside.

Finally, after another twenty-five minutes, the main man—consultant Dr Hacker himself—called her in and gave her a four-minute examination.

"All's well. Chemo on next Monday and Tuesday," he said brightly.

So, it was back to the Mercury Ward the following week, with yet more delays. It turned out Dr Hacker had marked Charlie's notes—and, it seemed, almost everyone else's—as needing another blood test "on the day". It meant the ward nurses had to take blood, rush it down to the test unit, get the results, get them OK'd by a doctor, take them to the pharmacy to get the chemo made up, return to pick it up, then get started. With a shortage of staff—just four nurses on duty that day—it meant one nurse was off the ward most of the time. Although she was working, Charlie heard later that she was ticked off for that later!

Having four hundred patients a week, the ward itself could be pardoned for any delays that happened and it showed Charlie just how hard-pressed and good the NHS staff were when it came down to frontline services. But it was very annoying when a two-hour session turned out to last six hours.

Charlie's hair had become dull and dead-looking and she began to get pains in her scalp. Then she noticed large tufts of hair on her pillow in the mornings. She suffered really badly from mouth ulcers and nose bleeds and was excessively tired all the time and slept a lot.

She was given acyclovir cream for the ulcers, and was offered a wig, although she didn't take it, preferring to just wear hats and scarves.

"That head scarf is like a symbol showing the women who are having treatment," said senior nurse Chris. "It's like a badge of courage."

"Courage?" asked Charlie.

"Yes. It shows you have the will to fight the cancer, and lets the world know about it." Chris smiled at her, obviously proud that he was part of the fight. "In any case, your hair will grow again."

Charlie had quickly slipped into the routine. Blood test and drip sessions in alternative weeks—it soon became the norm. The lively district nurses who now called on her to remove the infuser hanging from her waist after each session were all good fun. They joked and brightened up her day.

And it was not all bad news. By the fifth session, Charlie was well into the run of things: delays, blood tests, chemo sessions. At the Chemo Club, she enjoyed chatting to the others, and would walk round to their chairs pushing her stand with its bottles of drugs in front of her. She could not actually say she was enjoying it, but she was making the best of things as they were.

Everyone at the club seemed to appreciate the efforts she made, and Chris and the other nurses encouraged her. At one session, in fact, Chris persuaded her to sing for the others—a song from her last show. Everyone loved it, although Charlie felt her voice was a little off, and she managed to get everyone else singing a second song as well, with Chris proving he had a fine tenor voice. Despite everything else, Charlie felt really good.

That evening, she was exceptionally tired—more so than on any previous chemo evening—and slept in front of the television before going to bed earlyish. She was asleep by ten o'clock, and it turned out to be probably the best night's sleep she had enjoyed since first being diagnosed, waking just once at around 3 a.m. when the bottle—which usually didn't seem to be too much nuisance overnight—woke her up because it was hanging out of the bed and on the floor. Had she jerked it out of the wire? Was everything OK?

She pondered deeply, went to the loo with her eyes remaining shut, then went back to bed and straight off to sleep again.

Towards the end of the treatment, Charlie was constantly tired—more tired than she had ever been in her life—completely exhausted mentally and physically from the moment she woke up to the time she went back to bed. She literally wasn't capable of thinking. It was a deep-down tiredness, far worse than any she had ever known before.

But then it was over. Charlie completed her final session and said her goodbyes to the patients and staff in the Mercury Ward—all of them friends by then. She had survived the whole initial chemo treatment without too much bother.

She had to go back to the Mercury Ward for one last time to have the PICC removed, and the same nurse who had put it in, Widya, took her to a curtained-off bed and gently pulled it out. It was painless and only took a few minutes.

Between treatments, Charlie had tried again to ring Dane several times, but the phone was either unanswered or she got the answer-phone again. She was quite glad, because although she wanted to talk to him, she knew he would ask to meet her, and she did not want that as by now she looked a bit of a sight, not at all like the lively star of a West End show. She had sad eyes, her body was hunched, and she had a haggard, pinched face.

She was still having bad pains in the leg, which she was told was quite normal, and there was a large swelling below the knee, but a week after the end of the long chemo treatment, she went for another scan which showed the tumour had shrunk quite considerably. Mr Edwards, the surgeon, was delighted.

"A big success," he told her, and she knew he meant it.

But there were more tests and X-rays to come, and once again no time to call Dane. Finally, she was given a date for the operation four weeks later and was given an admittance form with details on how to report to the hospital.

# Chapter 16

# THE OPERATION

When it was first decided that Charlie had to go into hospital, Aaron had wanted her to have a room in a private clinic but she refused. She repeated that to the various doctors, and when, after the chemo, Aaron came back and once more asked if he could get her a private room, she refused yet again, insisting that she wanted to be in a ward with other people.

"I don't mind mixed wards either," she laughed.

Charlie, who was now looking more like her normal self, got the formal call to the hospital after the month was up, and duly reported to the hospital reception for the formalities before being admitted to her ward at just gone 7:35 p.m. She put on the open-backed hospital gown and the nurses duly gave her some routine checks. A notice above her bed read "Nil by Mouth", so she watched quietly as the ward busied itself with the early evening meal, pill-giving and the like.

There were eight beds in the ward—four on each side. It was one of about ten that branched off a long corridor, and Charlie's was the first on the right as you came in. Nurses hurried backwards and forwards from a central ward desk in the middle of the outer corridor.

All the beds in Charlie's section were filled, although most of the time the middle-aged woman in the third bed along on the other side simply sat on the edge of hers staring into space. Opposite Charlie was a very old woman who looked in a sorry state, and the others ranged from a teenager at the far end on her side through middle age to the old woman opposite.

Each bed had a "table" that was more like a tray on a wheeled frame that could be pulled across the patient's knees. There was an angle-poise lamp fixed to the wall over each, sockets and plugs for electrical or oxygen devices and a swing television set which could be pulled across in front of the patient.

The lights were dimmed early that first night, and Charlie fell into a deep sleep with nothing bothering her. Next morning, she woke at 7:15 with nurses bustling round, and she watched slightly enviously as the other patients had breakfast put before them on their tray-like bed tables. She would dearly have loved to have a cup of tea.

At around 8:20 a young male nurse stopped by her bed and gave her a pill—it turned out to be a "happy pill" that relaxed her immediately—and about forty-five minutes after that, an orderly came and wheeled her, still in her bed, along a corridor, into a lift, and down to the operating theatre area.

She was remarkably calm as she was wheeled down.

"It's like a first night," she told the male porter pushing the bed, then "directed" his steering—"left a bit, right a bit, straight on..."—as he pushed her into the lift.

"Yeah, a real opening night," joked the porter. "Surgeons would love to say that to patients, but they daren't. Some would take it the wrong way."

Charlie could not be upset at his cheerful manner.

In an outer room of the operating suite, Charlie's name and details were checked against her wrist bracelets—for some reason she now had two, both on the same wrist—and then she was wheeled into the anaesthetic room for an epidural.

"An epidural? Why? Am I having a baby?" she joked once more, still completely relaxed. Chatting to a nurse standing by her head about a dance film that was currently playing, she heard someone behind her saying the epidural needle was "about six inches in now". Then there was nothing.

It took just over two and a half hours for the operation to remove the primary tumour, and Charlie didn't feel a thing until she woke up.

As she slowly struggled back to consciousness with her eyes still closed, she could feel her heart pumping through her chest and she knew she was still alive. But her mind wondered.

"Does your heart still beat in heaven?" it asked her.

She opened her eyes and became aware that her leg was encased in a huge, fat dressing, with a cage over it for protection and with tubes and drips and draining bags hanging over the side of the bed. She was in the recovery room, and she was shivering with cold. She called out, and a bright young male nurse brought a small electric heater to put by the side of her bed to try to help. It didn't.

He told her not to move if possible and after a while an attendant came to wheel her silently back to the ward. She was very tired, and though she slept deeply she was woken every hour on the hour for nurses to check her pulse, temperature and to stick a needle into her lower body to see how far the epidural anaesthetic numbness had worn off. The nurses had to lift the leg with great care to clean it up.

The next morning, a medical team visited her to ask how she felt, and later Mr Edwards also came, sitting on a low stool by the side of the bed so his eyes were on a level with hers. He told her he had inserted a new titanium prosthesis inside the bone itself, which he said would make it as firm as the original.

"What I did was cut out the tumour and some bits round it, then I fixed up the leg so it should be almost as good as new, but without the nasty stuff growing inside," he told her. "Quite often the bone starts to regrow around the prosthesis, but even without that it should be as solid as a rock. Hopefully, unless my tape measure is wrong, I got it all back to the same length that it was."

"Will I be able to dance again?" asked Charlie.

"Sorry, I don't know. But I'd be lying if I didn't say I doubt if it will be to a professional level," said the surgeon in his calming, matter-of-fact way.

For the next week or so, Charlie had a series of ten drugs to take daily—usually in one session!—and had some strange dreams. Strange shapes floated in front of her eyes—her own "trip" dream— and one day she even had a fantasy in which she was positive she was taking part in a serious and superior quiz on some very obscure subjects to which she knew all the right answers even before the questions had been put. When Mr Edwards and his registrar made their daily call, she told them about it and said she didn't have any knowledge of the subjects and still didn't even now she was awake.

"I didn't even dream the questions first. I just gave the answers," she told them.

Mr Edwards smiled. "We'll have to give you something to get you to predict the lottery results," he said.

Charlie slept a lot in the days after the operation, only waking up when she was thirsty—which was often—or when she was woken to take her pills. When the nurses changed the dressings on her leg, she saw she had a scar down the whole length of it: inflamed, red, purple and black and with angry-looking stitches. The leg seemed a strange shape, although it looked better later when the stitches were removed and a back-plaster pack was securely bandaged to keep the leg rigid, but leaving the front open so the wound could be washed and dressed.

"Lucky you have a dancer's strong thigh muscle. It's helping hold the sling around the knee that's holding the tendons in place," said Mr Edwards. He continually explained everything that was happening, which Charlie found helpful and a comfort.

At first, she still had frequent bouts of sickness and was given painkillers and sedatives, and for a while she didn't feel like eating. She liked the thick hospital soups and survived on them. When she ate anything else, she would usually vomit. She was pale, thin, weak and worn out again.

In those early days after the operation, Charlie suffered several bouts of depression and her body would not always function properly. One day, she was half asleep when she realised she'd had an accident—the bed felt dirty and she woke up fully to call a nurse.

"Nurse, I've had an accident," she called.

Two nurses came immediately and helped her out of the bed—while one cleaned her, the other changed the sheets. It was all practical and non-emotional—no fuss, no bother, they'd seen it all before—and although Charlie felt immensely thankful, she was ashamed and kept very quiet for the rest of the day until the medical team shift changed.

She hated having the nurses give her bed baths, and soon managed to persuade them to let her wash herself—still in bed—from the waist up. But the nurses always had to clean her lower parts in case she knocked the leg.

After a while though, she began to feel more like her old self, and on the seventh day she took her first walk, with a physiotherapist and a nurse on either side of her, just a few yards along the main sixty-foot-long corridor, before collapsing back on the bed exhausted, but with a big grin on her face. After that, she was able to limp to a shower on the other side of the main corridor, wearing a large plastic case over her entire left leg. That was an improvement, and she began to look better, with the colour returning to her cheeks.

Back in the ward, the old lady in the bed opposite was still there. Charlie had often seen her face creased in agony and had given her a friendly smile when she looked up. The old lady responded. Charlie noticed that the old lady's visitors were always a man who was obviously her husband, with their son and daughter. The son was an exact replica of the father, the daughter identical to her mother. None of them ever seemed to say a word to the old lady.

Now, as she began to feel a bit better and was able to get out of bed on her own, Charlie often went across to speak to her. The old lady listed her complaints—cancer, diabetes, liver problems—and Charlie felt so sad at her plight, but inwardly felt better for her own "lesser" problems.

One day, Charlie was pleased when the hospital priest stopped for a chat, although she was not particularly religious. When he asked, "Do you mind if I talk?" she readily agreed. Apart from anything else, he was interesting and kept off the subject of religion, and the feeling of being wanted was good, and it passed time.

There was a Cockney male nurse who frequently cheered her up though—"Blimey, another bally dancer with a leg problem!"— and he was particularly chatty and would talk to Charlie about all manner of things.

"Oh, we've all got things wrong with us in here," he told her cheerfully one day. "Even me. I'm colour blind. I'd love to see more than four colours in a rainbow, but it's not to be. But I resent it because I would like to tell what colour your blood is. I mean, as you're such a big fillum star, are you really one of the blue bloods, the posh lot, or have you just got common-as-muck red blood like the rest of us?"

She laughed with him, not a bit insulted by his cheery, jokey way.

It was one of the few occasions her "stardom" was mentioned. At first the nurses did try to pay her special attention because of who she was, but they soon got used to that and began treating her like everyone else in the ward, especially after Charlie had directed them to other patients in need. The patients themselves, however, insisted on trying to talk to her about her film and stage life, the "glamour" of it all, the handsome co-stars. She discouraged them as much as possible, but there was always a newcomer who started the conversation again.

Things were not helped by her show biz visitors. There weren't too many of them, although a couple of the dancers from her last show turned up a couple of times, because the timings of matinees and evening performances worked against the hospital's strict visiting hours.

The floods of get-well cards that came in from fans every day also made Charlie out to be something special, although she tried not to be. She wondered how so many people knew she was ill, or how they found out what hospital she was in. She kept a couple of cards from friends on her bedside table, but after looking at the others—and replying if there was a heart-moving message in it—she gave most away to a charity volunteer to hang in other wards as decoration. She learnt later that several were sold as souvenirs because her name was mentioned on the card.

As well as Mr Edwards and his team, a young, cheery physiotherapist—who spoke of how she used to dance when she was six—came regularly. There were others, not always the same one, so she had no chance to build up any real rapport, but they were all intent on helping her learn to bend her knee and ankle, and generally get used to using the "new" leg.

In the early days, Charlie was helped to walk to the end of the long corridor and put in a wheelchair to be taken back to bed, but one day, when the physio went to get the chair, she tried to do it on her own and knocked herself out so badly she collapsed on the bed much to the consternation of the medical staff. It prolonged her stay in the hospital by two days.

She was often wheeled to a side ward to use a treadmill, and gradually the length of the walks down the corridor with the physio increased.

She still had a slight problem keeping her balance though and as the leg started to heal, she was taken in a wheelchair to a physio gym, where she practised walking while hanging on to parallel bars, and after a few days of that she had to practise going up a small gadget with four steps on each side to see how she could cope with them. It was like practising at the barre when she was studying ballet as a youngster.

She refused a walking stick, although to start with she often had to grit her teeth and lean against a wall to keep her balance.

As the "learning" progressed, Charlie felt much better in herself and began noticing things around the ward. For instance, she wryly observed that the surgical teams visiting the other patients in the ward used to arrive in a line with the consultant self-important and tallest at the front, the registrar—his number two—a bit shorter, and the rest decreasing in size and importance going down to the intern at the end. The consultants inevitably showed their influence by standing at the foot of the bed, picking up the patient's notes from the hook hanging on the front rail of the bed, then without ever looking at the patient imperiously asking how he or she was while still looking at the pad of medical notes. When given the answer "OK", Mr Big would pass the message back over his shoulder, to be relayed down the line in turn until the young intern at the back would make a note on a pad—later to be transferred by a nurse back to the notes held by the consultant.

Once, a nurse was chatting to one of the other patients when her consultant came in.

"What are you doing?" he demanded. "Haven't you something else to do rather than distract my patient?"

In Charlie's case, however, the team would visit her in a group, often sitting on her bed, friendly and chatty, with Mr Edwards, having got their report, himself turning up later on his own to see her. He had a military bearing that was at one and the same time formal and informal, and Charlie found out later that he had been a lieutenant colonel in the Royal Army Medical Corps and had seen frontline action somewhere in the Middle East. He was always relaxed, and he relaxed Charlie when he spoke to her. He was always candidly open and honest.

She noted too that while the other consultants stood towering over the front of the patients' beds, Mr Edwards came to the side of hers, and if there was no chair would actually squat down so he faced her eye to eye. He was much more friendly and less intimidating than the others.

Life though became boring in hospital as she got better. Although they tried to be friendly and chatted when they were doing things around the bed, the nurses were, in the main, far too busy to talk much. Charlie realised just how busy when she knocked a glass of orange juice over onto her bedside table and asked one of them if she could clear it. The nurse said she would be back "in a few moments", and when she had not returned after ten minutes or so, Charlie began to get angry, until she thought the nurse was probably saving someone else's life and mopped up the mess herself with some tissues. She noticed that when pairs of nurses would methodically make beds together, they did so without talking, each working like cogs in a robot. It was the only time they got to "relax".

She tried reading books, newspapers, magazines, but quickly lost interest in them. Once she pulled across the television set that hung on a swing bracket beside each bed to watch a ballet: Swan Lake. But she could not associate with it. She knew she wanted to dance, but at that particular moment she wasn't interested.

After the old lady opposite her disappeared one night, Charlie visited the other patients in the ward for a chat, but it did not really relieve the boredom of hospital life because many of them were either too ill or they gushed at her fame. Eventually, she extended the visiting to some of the other bays off the main corridor, but the patients in the other rooms also only wanted to talk about her star status and celebrity friends, so she stopped doing that. What she liked about the medical staff was that they just accepted her for who she was and treated her exactly like the other patients.

By now her hair was beginning to grow again, slowly, but the same colour as before.

"I noticed some of the male patients in the other wings are the same," she told Mr Edwards' registrar, "But their beards seem just as tough and they say they have to shave every day..."

"Ah, that's because beard hair is different from your top hair," he said, semi-serious and busied himself with her notes, a smile on his face. "Nothing for you to worry about personally."

Charlie got quite chatty with a young Polish girl who wheeled a trolley through the ward twice a day offering tea or other drinks. The girl seemed remote, but was delighted when Charlie greeted her one morning.

"Dzien dobry."

The girl looked wide eyed. "Oh, jak się masz?" she asked Charlie. The young girl jabbered something in Polish, and Charlie laughed.

"I don't know any more Polish," she said. "That's all I've been able to find out. I got a friend to look it up on a computer translation site!"

After that, the girl, obviously lonely, always stopped for a short chat in her broken English when she visited the ward.

Later during her stay, as her health improved, some of Charlie's old friends and colleagues now found time to visit her—sometimes having to "woo" the ward sister because they were out of hours. Aaron was one and Marguerite Johnson, the second lead in her film who had become a good friend. Marguerite insisted that when she left hospital, Charlie should come back to stay with her in her apartment.

"You'll need someone hefty to lift you in and out of bed," she joked.

Other visitors surprised her. Danny was one of the first—he cheered her up no end and sang a ribald song to one of the nurses—and Batty, the producer of her film, charmed everyone in the ward with his Old World courtliness.

It was about a week later that Charlie read a gossip column that said Dane had returned to America. Charlie surprised herself by not feeling any emotion at the news. It had happened several times before in her relationships with men. *Guess I only really love 'em when I can dance with them,* she thought.

Then late one evening, a little over three weeks later, she was told she could go home. She phoned Aaron to tell him, and the next morning Mr Edwards called for a farewell chat and gave her an urgent warning not to use the leg too much at first but to take things easily. She signed some forms, and on her discharge in the early afternoon, Aaron picked her up in a chauffeur driven car and took her back to Marguerite's apartment to hand her into the care of her friend.

# Chapter 17

# FINAL CHEMO

In no time at all, it seemed, Charlie was back for the final post-op spell of chemo. Remembering the lesson of the first series of sessions, Charlie turned up at the Mercury Ward wearing a blouse and sweater both with loose sleeves that could be rolled up easily.

She reported to the same sour-faced, over-busy receptionist, then followed the still familiar path to the waiting room with nurses hurrying everywhere, occasionally stopping to talk to one another, brisk, bustling, then calling in a patient into the doctor's room—the harassed doctors invariably trying to calm their patients by acting as though tomorrow would do.

Once again, she saw Dr Hacker, who asked her if she wanted to take part in another clinical trial which would mean extra weeks of chemo using the same three drugs as before but possibly with an extra couple depending on her response to the treatment. Having felt so bad in the first spell, Charlie once more declined. Dr Hacker accepted the refusal, but it was his nurse again who yet seemed quite cross about it.

After the session with Dr Hacker, Charlie was first of all sent for a CT scan, then she had a blood test, after which she returned to have the PICC line restored and the cannula taped back onto her right forearm. She still had a small scar in the crook of her elbow, left there after the first session of chemo, and although it was very small, hardly discernible unless you knew it was there, the Indonesian nurse Widya rubbed it to try to get rid of the mark before adding the gelatinous anaesthetic. When it wouldn't disappear, she selected another site a bit further over.

With the line fitted, Charlie was told to go away for three days while the clinic waited for results from the scan, then it was back into the same routine for the first of the new series of chemo treatments. There were to be six more of the fortnightly sessions this time, alternating as before with checks to see that her blood count had returned to a suitable level.

Between sessions, Charlie would see many different doctors sent in to check on her progress. One was Asian and introduced himself as Dr Hu.

"That way everyone will remember me if I make a mistake but won't know Hu to blame," he announced cheerfully.

Whoever it was, as before, there was either an instant "You're OK to carry on" or sometimes "Sorry, your white cell count is down. No chemo this week". It was heart-breaking when that happened.

When she reported to the ward for the first of the new sessions she found the same lead nurse, Chris, was still in the ward, and he welcomed her back with an enthusiastic hug. Charlie immediately felt part of the family.

"You might react the same way as last time or it may be different," he told her. "Everyone reacts in their own way. Some just sail through it all. Others are terribly ill, just as you were last time. There's no way of knowing."

Charlie looked round the ward and remembered it all clearly. The oval-shaped plastic bags hanging from hooks on the tall wheeled stands, two wires dripping down from each and then into the arms of the patients sitting patiently. They silently watched the drips of chemicals plop, pause, plop, pause, plop.

After that first session, the tiredness quickly returned, a deep-down fatigue in which she felt more exhausted than she had ever felt before. Wearier, she thought, than she had been even after a gruelling fourteen hours of non-stop rehearsal just before one opening night.

The next session was delayed because of a bank holiday, and during the long weekend Charlie simply stayed indoors, wallowing in her loneliness. It was not until the Tuesday of the third week that she returned for another white cell check-up. It turned out to be a disastrous morning.

Charlie got to the clinic early for the test, only to find the blood test unit was closed until 1:30 p.m.—an hour and three quarters after her appointment with the consultant. It was suggested she go to the main hospital's unit instead.

The nurse there was in a foul mood. There were two of them in the unit having to cover for the specialist cancer unit as well as their own patients. Charlie was the fifteenth and last of their "customers", but this "angel of mercy" got irritated by the guy in front of her—a confused ninety-year-old—because he didn't move fast enough into her room. She called Charlie in his place, telling her she didn't have time for "old buffers like that".

Then she couldn't find an artery. Charlie felt her poking around, pushing and prodding, and when she looked there was a noticeable pool of blood on her forearm.

She managed to refrain from saying what she thought of her "treatment", and eventually the nurse said she didn't have time and sent her back to the clinic to get one of the nurses there to take blood. Charlie went back, a nurse took blood without demur, and then she waited to see the consultant.

Another nurse came out after about thirty minutes or so and asked if she had had the CT scan. When Charlie told her that she had—with the date and time—she said the results seemed to have gone missing, so Charlie would have to wait until they found them.

When she was eventually called in, she saw a female doctor she had never seen before who said Mr Wyatt and his whole team would have to study the scan closer before the next clinic. She shook her head from side to side.

"Is there something wrong?" asked Charlie, apprehensive.

"No," said the doctor absently. "No, nothing wrong. But I think the experts should have a look."

"I thought you were an expert."

There was no answer, and Charlie was dismissed from the room.

Outside in the main waiting area again, Charlie found that the blood results had still not come through, and she was asked to wait again. Having been told it usually took about forty-five minutes after the blood was taken, she waited another sixty-five minutes—a total of eighty-five minutes from the blood-letting—before asking what was going on. A nurse told her to go home and wait for a phone call. That nurse was smashing and more understanding than many others having to do the admin work in the consultants' area. The trouble was there were always far too many patients and not enough working staff to help them while the consultants went about their oh-so-slow, but important, tasks.

Charlie finally got home at around 2 p.m., having gone out at 9:15 a.m., and the call came at 3:30. The tests, she was told, showed the blood count was low—no chemo that week—and another week before the next clinic. And that would just be to get another check.

By the Wednesday she was in a state of real deep-down despair—something she had not really experienced before. She felt really low mentally, and her brain was telling her that if "they" wanted her to be ill, she would be ill! It was a real body blow.

Although living with Marguerite, Charlie was, really, just extremely lonely.

Whether psychologically or because of the low white blood cell count—she called it her bloody cell count—she began to ache all over. Her arms, her shoulders, her legs, her chest. All ached, and she went to bed crying. When district nurse Babs Miller called the next day, Charlie told her over a cup of tea about the way she felt.

"I'm sure it wasn't this bad first time," she said.

"It probably was, but you've forgotten how bad it was," replied Babs softly. "Or it may just be there's an accumulation. You know, a build-up effect."

Charlie found she could relax with Babs, a dizzy-seeming girl who appeared completely scatter-brained, but who actually never missed a thing. She told Charlie she had started out working in a hospital but had never got on with the discipline or the plethora of managers there and had often been in trouble with the matron or ward sister.

"It's much easier doing this job, getting out and about on my own," she laughed. "You get more cups of tea as well."

During her visits, they spoke of several things, and Babs showed Charlie photos of her young daughter.

"I wish I could get her to settle down to do something positive," she said one day. "She's a bright kid, interested in things, but she watches too much telly."

They discussed it casually for a moment or two, then Charlie had a sudden idea. "Why don't you get her to go to dancing classes?" she asked. "That could be something special for her."

Babs smiled. "Sounds like a good idea," she said.

It helped Charlie's mood, and by Thursday she was over the depression and began to feel like a human being again. But the fact remained: it would be a whole month between the first and the second sessions of the new course of chemo. An eternity.

When Charlie did eventually get back to the ward, there was a certain amount of uncertainty in her mind. It was almost as if she was just starting treatment from the beginning, although she obviously knew what was going to happen. It all seemed a bit unreal—it was probably the break in routine after so many months that made it feel so different. Or was it wondering if a month's break would make any difference to the overall treatment result?

In the event, things went along as usual, although along with the normal anti-nausea pills, she was given five injection syringes to be given by the district nurses on consecutive days after the start of that second session. She was told they would help boost the white cells.

For some reason, the first of the injections gave Charlie every symptom normally associated with the chemo itself! There was extreme tiredness and listlessness, nausea, pains in her leg and knee—the reason why she'd gone to see her GP at the start of it all— loose bowel movements, a permanent dry and "metallic" mouth and tongue, catarrh and a vague blockage in the throat, a return of the slight nasal bleeding, tingling fingers almost all the time, and "pinpricks" in her feet and legs. There were also foot cramps, and she actually staggered on occasions.

Towards the last of the injections, she had a tight chest, breathlessness, and aches in the shoulders, and she panicked a bit. She decided to phone the clinic to check, and they told her that as she had to visit the clinic in any case, she should leave it and let them check her out and, if necessary, give her the final injection there.

In the ward on her next visit, they asked Charlie about the chest pains and called a doctor to sound her out with a stethoscope. He prodded and tapped and finally said it all seemed all right. It was, he said, just a "blip" and all seemed well.

"Tell us if it comes back," he added as he hurried away.

The session continued as before, but on the second day Charlie noticed she only had one drip instead of the usual two, and wondered if this was another way to help the white cell count built up. Charlie did ask a nurse, but although she said she'd check, they both forgot. When she remembered later, she forgave the nurse. They were all so dedicated, hard worked and over worked.

Her reaction this time seemed a little easier, though just a little. There was only a very vague fingertip tingling and a fairly persistent metallic dry taste in the mouth—although her appetite stayed as strong as ever, and Charlie was putting on weight like mad—but the severe tiredness seemed perhaps a bit worse than usual and in the two days after the chemo she felt really out of things, mentally and physically. Extreme lethargy being the words. But it was bearable.

A week later, it was back for yet another white cell blood count. This time, it was sluggish despite the booster pills, and she was told the remaining four chemo sessions would have to be delayed by three weeks to allow her blood to build up. It was yet another kick in the stomach—the worst thing that had happened so far. It felt like the end of the earth, and Charlie was completely shattered by the "disaster" and went home in the depths of despair.

Although she disliked them, the chemo sessions were a break in Charlie's life of loneliness—fairly brief respites. But that was all. They were hard work that simply took over for a time, and although working to repair her body did not mend her mind.

It was so bad that it soon began to affect her mental health and she became dejected and moody. She didn't sleep well, was listless, without any energy, ambition or the will to dig herself out of her slough of despair. She had no incentive to get out of bed.

For days she didn't leave her room, and life was simply a sad routine of drifting from one day to the next.

Then after three or four weeks of nothing, she woke up in the early hours one morning with her mind going round and round. She was snug in bed, but she felt cold and didn't want to look at a clock or get up. As she lay half under the duvet, a sudden thought came to mind—a serious thought. *Oh my God, am I going mad? Is my mind going?* she reflected. It was raining, the drops lashing against the bedroom window, and the room was gloomy. *I think I am going mental,* she thought. *I'm getting a mental condition.*

Half asleep, she thought about her emotional behaviour since leaving the show, and instinctively she knew she would have real problems if she didn't do something to occupy her mind. She knew she had to pull herself together, and she wanted to get back to work: to go to auditions to try to find another show.

She didn't really feel physically well enough to go back to work though, but in her own mind the omnipresent feeling of dancing in the show was always with her. She missed the routine of going to the theatre daily, either for a rehearsal or a performance. She tried going to the cinema, but the film didn't interest her, and she joined the audience of another live theatre show. Both times she was conscious on the way out that everyone round her had someone to talk to, to discuss the film or play with and to keep the mood of the entertainment for a little longer.

She went to restaurants, but once again she had no one to talk to. She had no friends outside the theatre, and they were invariably working. She had no boyfriend, no family, no one in her life. She went to supermarkets so she could at least chat to the checkout girls or boys. Although they were often cheery, she knew there was no personal connection.

Apart from Babs and Marguerite, who was out most of the time, Charlie was hardly seeing anyone. She was lonelier than ever before, and the days passed slowly between the chemo sessions.

At the sessions themselves, Charlie tried to read books as she sat with the wires in her arm, but it was difficult to concentrate and during the long, tiresome spells she would spend long periods just watching the drip, drip, drip of the innocuous-looking, mainly colourless drugs fed into her body. She remembered she had watched the other patients reacting in that same robotic way when she returned for the first session of the "new" chemo. The dripping had a curious, mind-numbing fascination—a bubble would form in one of the bags hanging above her, would stay for a few seconds, then the liquid would plop down and into the tube to her arm as another droplet began to form.

Throughout the whole process of alternating blood checks and chemo sessions, there would always be two men sitting in a corner, wires connecting them to the machines as the drugs dripped into their arms, talking earnestly on some obscure subject far from medical matters, intimate as only two long-term illness sufferers can be. Young women looking scared, middle-aged women looking tired, the elderly looking resigned.

While waiting to see the doctors for blood test results, there was always a whole mass of people in the waiting room, all looking just scrubbed and anxiously ready to see the consultant to get the results of their tests, but she never recognised any of them in the chemo ward.

Her hair—which had by now regrown almost to shoulder length—began to fall out again. Once more, Charlie was close to tears, and the feeling of weary listlessness was exacerbated when she went to the clinic again the following week to be rechecked.

This time Charlie had the blood test forms with her and when she started the visit by calling in to what she by now called the Vampire Unit for the ritual blood-taking, the nurses couldn't have been sweeter or gentler.

She went to wait outside the Great Man's clinic, and was eventually called in. Her papers had arrived at the right place, and this time she saw a younger doctor she'd never seen before. He discussed Charlie's former work as a dancer and seemed particularly interested in her singing.

"I always wanted to be a singer. The new Caruso," he told her.

Charlie played along with it, conscious that there were other patients patiently waiting outside, and finally the doctor studied her notes. By then, a nurse had brought in the blood test results, and after looking at them he told Charlie that the readings were so low he had no alternative than to put off the next session of chemo again.

One drug in particular, he said airily, acted on the bone marrow and resulted in a loss of red blood cells causing anaemia. Overall, there was a decline in white cells and a depletion of the platelets that circulated in the blood helping growth and could lead to the formation of blood clots.

It was meaningless to Charlie. All she could absorb was that the next session had been delayed yet again and she felt like screaming.

"I'm sorry," he told her, but she could see that she was just another body that had to be seen, given a message, then dismissed.

For a while, Charlie began to blame the medics for all the delays, but then she reasoned it was her own body that was reacting badly. She took several mental deep breaths and got on with it. Finally, it was on to session four. At least, she thought, that would take her past the half way stage.

After a satisfactory blood test, she returned to the Mercury Ward where the nurses checked on her regime of drugs and told her that because of the symptoms she had shown before, it might be better if she took a couple of paracetamol instead before the session, telling her it might be just as helpful. Apart from the usual mid-afternoon tiredness, that was that. She was two-thirds of the way through.

It was not all bad, gloomy news though. One day she was resting at home in Marguerite's house, her feet stretched full length in front of her as she sat on a settee, when there was a ring at the doorbell. She slowly swung her feet down and went to open it. Aaron, her agent and producer, was standing there.

"I was just passing…" he said.

Charlie invited him in and offered a cup of coffee.

"A small tea, perhaps," he replied, and then he followed her into the kitchen as she filled the kettle and prepared the drink.

"I just wanted to see how you're getting on," he told her.

Charlie looked at him over her shoulder. "Oh, fine," she replied. "It's so nice of you to ask. I feel quite forgotten."

She got biscuits from a cupboard and prepared to put them on a plate.

"Don't bother with a plate. We can eat them from the packet," said Aaron.

Charlie smiled. "Just like rehearsals," she replied, her eyes twinkling.

When the tea was ready, Aaron insisted on carrying the two cups into the living room, and they sat side by side on the settee.

"You know, you're not forgotten. Everyone's asking about you," he said.

"Dane?"

There was an embarrassed silence. "Well, most people," said Aaron lamely. He busied himself dunking a biscuit in the tea, and the moment was broken when it collapsed in two and one sodden half of it floated in the cup.

"Nothing changes," laughed Charlie.

They nattered nothings to and at each other for half an hour or so before Aaron left. Charlie felt much happier after the visit. It cheered her up no end.

District nurse Babs dropped in later that same evening to tell Charlie that she'd followed up her idea and her daughter had indeed enrolled in a dancing class.

"She loves it," laughed Babs. "I just wish I could get her home sometimes to watch TV now!"

Charlie was delighted that she had been able to get someone else interested in dancing. Teaching young people was something she had vaguely thought might be something she could do when she "grew old".

For a while after that day Charlie was back to her solo exist-ence—merely plodding along with her mind mostly in neutral from day to day.

Then she was back to the chemo grind. Charlie had the usual blood test, the doctor said her white cells seemed OK, and the chemo could go ahead the next week. Charlie immediately felt bet-ter, and the next day there was not a symptom in sight.

But despite the bustle of life in the hospital when she went for the chemo sessions, Charlie's desolation was still the norm. When she attended the sessions, she was surrounded by people, but even though they were all incredibly friendly, the nurses and occasional junior doctors were all too busy to really unbend and take her into their lives, while the other patients were, like her, too bound up in their own unhappy plight to become a deep part in her life. It was all too unreal to be real life—recurring bouts of rush and bustle in between the realities of her aloneness.

Then, miraculously it seemed, Charlie was preparing for the final session. All the way through her second series of sessions she had been counting them down. After the first it was "one-sixth", after the second "one-third" and so on. Now it was the last. At least, she hoped it would be the last session.

During the week leading up to it, she was extremely lethargic, staggered when she stood up, nauseous. She was apathetic, had aching legs and feet like never before, tingling fingers most of the time... although her appetite remained remarkably healthy!

Then on the day of what she hoped would be the final session, a deep, deep depression set in again.

"I don't think I've ever been so depressed so often," she told Chris. "I used to be so optimistic..."

"Don't worry too much," replied Chris, encouraging her. "It often happens at the end of the course. You'll feel better after to-morrow."

And she did. That last day went well, and finally the chemo was all over. The PICC line was removed for the last time, and although Charlie felt extremely tired, everything seemed fine. As she left the clinic, almost all the nurses told her they'd miss her, although they let another "farewellee" go without a word!

"You've become part of the family," said Chris as he kissed her on the cheek.

And Widya later added to the special farewell. "Chris wouldn't tell you, but I know how pleased he was that you didn't play the big film star and that you bothered to help some of the others," she said.

Charlie supposed she should have felt elated after completing the final session, maybe even thankful it was more or less over, but there were no feelings like that at all. Nothing. Apart from a nagging feeling growing in her mind that because of the pains in her feet, her dancing days might be delayed for a long, long time.

And although the actual treatment was over, she still had to wait a couple of weeks for the final screening and check, and the hopeful sign-off.

The anticipated "couple of weeks" waiting for the scan turned into five and a half weeks of anxiety. Charlie's general health varied and she ran the whole gamut of physical feelings. One day she would be listless and achy, the next more or less fine. Most of the various symptoms of the chemo—the metallic taste in her mouth, the nausea—slowly faded away, although she still got tired fairly easily, very deeply, and very quickly.

Gradually, things seemed to be moving in the right direction though. Her hair was back to normal, slightly lighter than it had been—a colour Charlie liked—and the only symptom after a few weeks was the lack of sensitivity in her fingertips and toes, although sometimes she imagined the feeling was slowly starting to return. She had been told the feeling would probably go away eventually, but when it didn't it began to get to her down and she ranted and railed about it internally. All to no avail, of course.

The wait for the scan began to prey on her mind too, and when it got to the stage that she felt she could no longer wait, Charlie chased the scanner unit to be told they did not have any available slots and she would have to carry on waiting. But after a second phone call a couple of days later, she was told she could have the scan on the following day if she wanted! She rang Mr Wyatt's secretary and arranged to see him a week later to get the results.

The scan itself went without incident, and Charlie was left with an ever-increasingly tense seven days waiting for the result.

# Chapter 18

# AFTER THE TREATMENT

**B**ack home, Charlie forced herself to go for occasional walks, but her legs hurt too much for her to go very far, and so eventually she bought herself an exercise bike for the times she did not feel like strolling through the streets. But the bike was very much second choice, especially after her dancing. Charlie did not use it all that often. She either forgot or could not be bothered.

As she drifted back to health, life went on around her tirelessly, and Charlie watched it all but did not feel a part of it. Depression was always somewhere around her, and it wasn't helped when one day she was in her local supermarket and a stranger walked up to her, looking at her in a funny way. Charlie tried to ignore it.

"Sorry to bother you, but I was a great admirer of you and your shows. I heard about your illness..." said the woman, and when Charlie muttered a quiet thanks, she went on to show real sympathy. "I loved your singing. Such lovely songs... Oh, what's your name?"

It amused Charlie for a while, but the humour soon wore off.

Then *the* day. Her final check. She arrived at the clinic dead on time for the appointment, only to have a haggard, rushed-off-her-feet nurse tell her there was a two-hour delay! Charlie resigned herself, and waited, getting more and more anxious and with everything she possessed aching. Finally, after an hour and a half, she was called in.

Another doctor she had never seen before came in, sat down, apologised for the delay, and told her, "We've never met before, so I'll have to get to know you from your notes," he said. And he began reading—almost to himself, "Hmm, scan is perfectly clear..."

Charlie didn't hear any more. All of a sudden, all the aches and pains of just a few minutes earlier had disappeared. She felt more than two hundred percent fine.

The doctor went into detail. The scan showed everything was normal, and Charlie's files would be returned to her surgical team who would eventually call her back to see how she was getting on. Despite her euphoric state, to Charlie it just seemed never-ending.

She was told she had to have regular after-checks with CT scans for five years—the first three months after the end of the chemo, then every six months, and finally annually.

Charlie listened with mixed-up feelings. She was pleased, of course, but she suddenly knew she had to make decisions—possibly unpleasant decisions—about her future.

She had an immense feeling of relief. "Thank you," she said, starting to stand up. "I could kiss you for that..."

The doctor seemed to push back in his chair. "It's, er, nothing," he muttered, embarrassed. "Delighted. We like to keep track of our patients. Make sure their bodies aren't doing anything naughty," he told her with a sudden smile.

"Naughty? At my age?" she laughed. "Or do you mean like the tingling in my fingers? And feet?"

"Don't worry about that. It's just that the nerve endings have been damaged by the chemo, maybe even killed off. It could go on for goodness knows how long. Another two weeks, two months, possibly even two years before the nerves rebuild themselves," said the doctor. "It could—"

"Does that mean I won't be able to dance until it's gone?"

"Well, I was going to say that the numbness could go on for the rest of your life," continued the doctor. "It has been known!!"

The words definitely ended with two exclamation marks.

*The rest of my life? They don't tell you that bit when they mention the possible side effects when you start the chemo*, thought Charlie, although she didn't say anything.

The doctor gave her what he thought was a reassuring smile, but which actually looked to Charlie more like a knowing leer.

"Anyway, things seem OK for now, so you can go off and get on with the rest of your life," he added, standing and holding out his hand to shake hers. He smiled again, friendly, relaxed.

"Get on with my life... that'll be nice," she said. "But my life is dancing. If the tingling does go on for the rest of my life, does that mean I'll never be able to dance again?"

"Hmmph," was the doctor's reply.

It was a bit of a shock, but the only positive news Charlie was really interested in was the scan was clear. She would never know if the chemo had actually cleaned anything up, or whether the precautionary treatment was just that—a precaution. It could have been that her body did it all by itself, or that the initial operation had taken out everything bad that needed to be taken out, but whichever way it was, her knee felt fine and there was a great relief all round.

Three weeks later, Charlie had to report back to her GP. She told him of the pins and needles that still affected her fingertips, toes and under her feet.

He listened, nodding, then told her, "It's called peripheral neuropathy. The chemo you had kills off the nerve endings, and they have to regrow."

"Yes, I was told that. But no one will tell me how long that will take."

"Oh, you could have it for the rest of your life," replied the doctor nonchalantly, repeating the information.

Charlie went away pondering. She had heard it before, but the doctor's words were still uncomfortable. She knew she couldn't dance with the neuropathy.

No longer dance? At least, in the way she had before. It didn't bear thinking about.

She thought, instead, of all the moments in her life when she had danced: as a six-year-old on stage, her first shows, the West End, Broadway, the Royal Variety show. Now it could be over.

She felt she should cry, but her eyes were dry. A feeling of opposition came over her, and the thought was still in her mind when she got home, still unsure how she felt.

"I'll never be able to dance again." It stayed in her mind as she sat with a cup of tea. "Ah well," she finally told herself. "I suppose it's better to have had the chemo than to have ignored it. But what if I can't dance anymore? What if it doesn't go away?"

The depression of her loneliness overcame her once more.

It was about a week later that Charlie read a newspaper gossip column that said Dane had opened in a new play in America, and it surprised her that she did not feel any emotion at the news. It had happened several times before in her relationships with men.

She was still living in Marguerite's apartment, where her friend was determined to look after her—Charlie felt mothered at every step. She was definitely being pampered.

Aaron called one day in a huge limousine to drive her to see Mr Edwards for a farewell chat, and the surgeon once again smiled as he gave her an urgent warning not to use the leg too much at first but to take things easy. She signed some release forms before Aaron drove her home again,

Back at Marguerite's flat, Aaron ushered her in, but accidentally dropped some items he was carrying and bent to pick them up. He grunted as he stood again.

"You must grow taller as you get into your eighties," he said. "The floor is a lot further away than it used to be."

When he kissed her goodbye, Charlie felt the stubble on his face, although he was apparently clean shaven, and automatically felt her own face to see if it was as lined and creased as his.

Marguerite clucked around her like a mother hen—"More like a grandmother hen the way you're carrying on," said Charlie—and wouldn't let her do anything, but soon a district nurse called on what was to be the first of an every two days' series of visits to check on the leg and its dressings and told her a little exercise would be a good thing. Then Charlie got a letter fixing yet another CT scan before she went back to see the chemo consultant.

It showed her the treatment had not yet completely finished.

Without the chemo appointments, Charlie quickly slipped back into her life of utter seclusion.

She was alone and lonely for most hours in her day, but apart from that Charlie slept, she woke, she ate. She did housework, went shopping and joked with the checkout girls in the nearby supermarket. Sometimes she read a book, but she was very lonely.

Depression was always somewhere around her.

# Chapter 19

# REBUILDING A LIFE

nd so, it was over.

At first, district nurses she didn't know called to keep an eye on her, but then it settled down to just Babs twice a week. She and Charlie got on marvellously together, and it became a routine that Babs would stop off from her daily routine visits for cups—always plural—of tea when she called.

They were of an age, and the tales would flow from Babs.

"Have I told you about when I was in a hospital, there was a ward sister..."

"Can't tell you her name, but there's one of my patients I visit near here..."

And they would both collapse in fits of giggles or peals of laughter.

Laughter, as Babs knew, was one of the best forms of recovery, and Charlie blossomed under it, slowly, with the always cheery Babs and their cups of tea, jokes, and laughter. Months after the end of her treatment, Charlie began to pick up her life again.

Slowly, things started to heal. But she still had a long scar down the side of her left leg—from slightly above the knee down to the ankle—and she found it difficult to walk. She grew frustrated with other things too like when a piece of paper dropped and she bent to pick it up. Because of the fuzziness she still had in her fingertips, she could not grasp it and she shook her hand in aggravation and tried again, this time able to lift the paper although she could not feel it. She often flexed her fingers—her whole hand—to try to get feeling back into them.

On some days her entire skin felt itchy, as if she had small spots all over, although none were there.

The feeling in her hands was peculiar. At times, the fuzziness extended through her fingers and into her palms, at others it stayed in the fingertips only. She often felt an icy cold patch in one spot or another—a feeling of freezing cold on the inside of the hands although the outside felt normal.

There were similarly unfeeling feelings in the soles of her feet and toes as well. It felt as if she was walking on a rubber pad. And apart from the pain underneath her feet, her ankles began to swell so that by the time she went to bed each night they would hurt and feel as though there was a thick crepe bandage tight around them both. They always settled by morning, but would often be replaced by a piercing pain at the base of each big toe, between them, and the toes next to them.

She recalled what she had been told: the pins and needles in her hands and feet "could go on for the rest of your life". She smiled wryly at the thought, and steeled herself to the fact that, although she hated the idea, she would only be able to return to dancing in the far, far, far-away distance. Whenever that feeling came, she made herself think of something else fairly quickly.

There were many days that were better than others, and on those days, she literally gritted her teeth and tried short walks. But although she tried in the empty apartment while her friend Marguerite was out, she was not able to dance.

The idea that she would *never* be able to dance recurred more frequently, and recuperating at home in Marguerite's apartment in West London became a miserable time for Charlie. Not because of Marguerite, but because she felt low, uncomfortable and at times despairingly sad.

"No one ever calls from the show," she complained. "It's so disappointing, disheartening." She never thought that Dane might call.

Marguerite gave her a pale smile. "Show casts are like that," she replied. "They're like a huge friendly family while the run is on, but as soon as it closes, all of us gypsies go about our business separately looking for a new family."

Babs kept insisting that she should try more walking—exercise, she said, would do Charlie good—but it was too painful.

One day, her old boyfriend Peter Mitchener, who had taken over the leading role starring opposite her in her first show *That Girl Next Door*, called to see how she was getting on. He did not tell her that he had bumped into Marguerite, who had told him how lonely Charlie was feeling.

They swapped memories, and although Charlie took care not to mention their feelings for each other before he had been rejected for the filming of the show, the visit cheered her up. They had coffees, then a glass of wine, and smiled a lot.

Finally, after about an hour and an half, Peter hauled himself to his feet.

"Got to go," he said casually. "Time to pick up the wife."

Charlie didn't know what to say. She felt as if her jaw had dropped and that she stood there with her mouth gaping.

"Didn't you know? I got married eighteen months ago. Thought you might have heard about it on the grapevine. A childhood sweetheart I suppose you could say. We went to school together."

Charlie still could not manage a word.

"We're expecting our first baby," added Peter.

For some reason the news was upsetting for Charlie. "Oh, I hope..." But she felt very down after Peter had left.

Then, some three months after the chemo treatment had ended, Charlie got a letter asking her to return to St. Mary's Hospital for the first of her post-op CT scans. She was given two dates: the first for the scan, and the second about a week later to get the result.

She went along on the first day not really knowing what to expect and was told that to start with she had to drink a cup of liquid every ten minutes.

"Do you want orange or lemon?" asked the receptionist, who, after Charlie had requested lemon, produced a plastic cup and a one-litre bottle containing a very pale-coloured and insipid-tasting liquid.

About halfway through the six cups, Charlie was called to a small curtained room at the back where a cannula was fitted to her right wrist, almost as in the chemo days.

After the hour, Charlie was called in for the actual scan, and some sort of highly coloured dye was injected into the cannula to highlight the pictures of the scan. The scan itself took just ten minutes, then Charlie had to wait for a while to have the cannula removed and was told she shouldn't leave the hospital for another hour in order to get over the effects.

In the event she went straight home feeling fine, and a week later turned up at the hospital's Mercury Ward to see Beth Whitehead, a specialist nurse consultant who was part of Dr Hacker's department. She seemed very severe when Charlie first walked apprehensively into her room.

"Hmm," said the nurse ominously, reading from some notes before looking up and facing Charlie eye to eye. "Well, you'll be pleased to hear everything's OK so far. You're doing well."

She gave Charlie a reassuring smile. "Nothing showed up in the scan, so off you go. I'll see you again in about six months or so. We'll send you a letter."

Charlie felt immediate relief. "What about the fuzziness in my fingers and feet?" she asked. "I've still got it. Will it go away?"

Nurse Whitehead shook her head. "You just can't tell," she replied. "We always hope so, but it depends on all kinds of things. I'm afraid you've just got to put up with it and pray."

It was the same story, but despite her apparent sternness Charlie felt she could trust the nurse.

With the follow-up procedure now established, Babs told Charlie she had to wind up her visits as she was now officially "off the list".

"I'll be going off on a senior management course in a couple of weeks anyhow," she said on the day after Charlie's visit to Beth Whitehead.

Charlie was delighted for her, although Babs said that even though the promotion would eventually be good for her, she would have to take a big drop in money during the six-month course. She promised to keep in touch.

Two days later, Marguerite unexpectedly landed two key roles: one in a new West End show and the other in a film to be shot at the same time. It meant she would be out of the way for most of the time. What with that and the end of Babs' visits, Charlie felt alone and an even deeper feeling of depression came over her.

In a desperate mood, she dropped in to see Aaron at his office for a reassuring chat. He had originally been her producer, and when success had started to come, he had taken over as her agent to save money. Now he was established as both a producer and agent in a swish new office and was building up his team with several younger dancers and singers. Despite the fact that he was also busy with a new show he was preparing, he was surprisingly gentle and considerate as he invited her in and called for coffee. With the drink growing cold in front of her, Charlie poured out her feelings of loneliness and doubts following on her illness.

"You just gotta play it like a role, like the—" He stopped. He was going to say "like the dying swan" but realised in time. "Like the girl in your film," he finished lamely.

Charlie managed a wry grin. She too had automatically thought of the dying swan in Swan Lake.

Aaron heard her out and gave her some comforting thoughts. But he was obviously preoccupied, and Charlie stood to leave.

"No matter what, I'll always stick with you," said Aaron as he saw her to the door. "Feel free to talk to me. Ask for anything..." He grinned. "Except more money!"

As Aaron went back into his office, his wife, who had once been his unpaid secretary and was sitting in the outer office, gave Charlie what was for her a rare smile.

"I know he's too busy to talk at the moment, even to me, but he cares about you. He really cares," she said.

Charlie went out feeling just a little better, although the mood of depression was still with her. As she made her way back through the streets to Marguerite's flat with nobody even looking at her, she had thoughts of moving out of the impersonal city and returning to the countryside where she had grown up.

As the feeling grew over the days, she began actively looking for a house away from the hustling London streets.

# Chapter 20

# TO THE COUNTRY

She had lived in London through all her working life and felt she was really a Londoner, but as Charlie looked around for a new home, she fell in love with the unaccustomed peace of the countryside. After delighting in the changes of the area from her former homes, she was musing over it in one small town teashop when she thought of the old saying, "When a man is tired of London, he is tired of life." *The eighteenth century writer Samuel Johnson, was it?* she asked herself.

No matter who wrote it, she pondered, he was wrong.

"More like the man who is tired of London wakes up when he sees the delights of the British countryside." *Or a girl come to that,* she thought.

As she continued trying to rebuild her new life she began going further out of London, and eventually saw a house in the small village of Tilstead in the countryside about forty miles south of the capital. The name on the gate called it Bluebell Cottage, and looking over the gate, Charlie could see why. There was a vast mass of those flowers that made the garden literally a sea of blue.

It was the garden that appealed to her. She had never had a garden, although her parents had a small strip at the back of their house, and when Charlie first saw Bluebell Cottage she was taken with the mass of multi-coloured flowers everywhere round it.

There were big bushes and shrubs as well, and they made a beautiful surround for the house. It was a low two-storey building with a deep inverted V roof, double-glazed casement windows on the ground floor and dormer windows jutting from the roof upstairs. It had ivy growing up the walls on three sides.

The surrounding area looked interesting as well. There was a pub at the far end of the road, and a low working men's club opposite. Most of the houses in the road, Pond Street, were detached and all looked well cared for. Charlie liked the whole effect from the start.

An estate agent's board was stuck in grass outside the garage driveway, and after getting no answer to her knocks at what turned out to be the back door, she walked into the garden to take photos of the place with her mobile. As she left, she took a picture of the board intending to contact them as soon as she could.

When she did phone the next day, she was quoted a price for the house, and although she had big savings from her time both on stage in London and New York and especially from making her film, it was too high. Disappointed, she hung up and wondered what to do next.

Over the next five days, Charlie did more touring and house hunting without any success. Then she went back to take another look at Bluebell Cottage, and felt so at home with it that she rang the estate agent again determined to plead with him to lower the price. That turned out to be unnecessary because, as she found out later, the occupier was a sick old lady living on her own, and her son had become desperate to move her out and into a residential home where she would get the medical help she needed.

When she was asked if she would improve her bid and say how much she was prepared to pay, Charlie took a chance and repeated her original offer—still only two-thirds of what the agent had hoped to get. The agent said he would check and phone her back.

That return call surprisingly came within the next hour and Charlie's offer was accepted. She agreed to go into the agent's office the next day to sort out the details and to sign anything that was necessary.

The agent proved to be an unctuous character that Charlie didn't like at all, but after going through a few details, they orally agreed the sale. The one other thing Charlie got out of their meeting was the fact that she really needed a solicitor or a conveyancer—a specialist lawyer dealing mainly in house sales—to act for her to sort out all the complex matters involved.

A quick visit to the local branch of her bank gave her the name of a local solicitor, and she once again made an appointment and went to see him.

Thomas Jones looked younger than Charlie had expected, but he was friendly and seemed to know what he was about. He knew the estate agent, and he told her he could act as both legal eagle and conveyancer and said she could leave things to him.

It didn't take Thomas long to get into action. He rushed in a surveyor, who official exchange of contracts and notified the Land Registry to notify them of the sale and get the title register. He wrote to Charlie advising a home insurance firm and suggesting she use it, then he organised services like gas, electricity and water. He even fixed up with a local milkman to deliver to the house three days a week.

While he was doing all that work, Charlie herself returned to the local bank and arranged for her account to be transferred from the London branch. Along with her savings, the annuity she had taken out when she started her professional career seemed to cover most things, but she also got the sympathetic manager to agree to a large overdraft should she need extra funding.

Thomas kept Charlie informed of his actions all the way through—either by letter, email, messages or phone calls—and sent her the various forms that needed to be signed. From the start, he tried to explain all the inexplicable ways and methods of the law as he set about winning her possession of Bluebell Cottage.

Eventually, he posted a copy of the final contract, largely filled with "whereases" and "wherebys" which she had to sign, and then finally he phoned to announce that he'd just about finished. Despite his speed, it had taken Thomas four months to reach completion.

It was a bright, sunny October morning when Charlie met him at the house and he handed over two sets of keys.

"Is that it?" asked Charlie. "It's all mine? Nothing else to do?"

Thomas shook his head slightly. "No, nothing more. I managed to get you exemption from stamp duty as you're a first-time buyer, so that's it," he said, smiling.

Then, still with the smile on his face, he added, "You are a first-time buyer, aren't you? I hope so. I've signed all the official documents saying you are, and I've told everyone. If not, well, possibly we'll share a cell."

They both laughed.

"Come in," said Charlie. "If there's a kettle, we can have a cup of tea."

And so, three days later, Charlie moved in to Bluebell Cottage. While Thomas had been working, she had bought furniture and some of the hundreds of things she knew she would need: cups, saucers, plates, pots and pans and the like. She could have transferred the fitments from her home in London, but it was easier to buy new and she was not particularly sentimental about things like that. She didn't realise for a while that new furniture does not carry personal history like the pieces in family homes.

The move itself was relatively simply, and within half an hour Charlie had a call from her immediate neighbour Linda Cummings. Linda was friendly, about ten years older than Charlie, and asked if there was anything she could do to help. Charlie said there wasn't anything immediate, and asked if Linda wanted a cup of tea. Linda refused and said she had to hurry off to work. She ran an estate agency business with her husband, although surprisingly they had not seemed to be involved in the sale of Bluebell Cottage.

"Another time, soon," she said.

It was, though, the last time Charlie saw her for quite a few weeks.

# Chapter 21

# LONELY

It took Charlie time to adapt to country life. She didn't know anyone, and although many people nodded to her when she went out for short walks round the neighbouring lanes and fields, she still felt apart from everyone.

The isolation was even more intrusive than it had been in London—there was no underlying noise from traffic, nor the continual background hum that always hung over everything in the city. To try to counter that, Charlie turned the television on as soon as she got up in the morning, and in most cases didn't turn it off until she went to bed. She didn't actually watch very much—it was just a steady background noise. Human voices droning on.

As well as everything else, as much as she liked and enjoyed Bluebell Cottage it was all still so strange to Charlie with new furniture that was not like she was used to—pieces usually found in family homes with a personal history.

Trying to get some sort of relief, she went to the village pub, the Vixen Hunter, for an evening meal and sat there alone feeling like the outsider she was. Even when Linda and her husband Eric came in, there was no comradeship. They had a short chat with her, but they knew and were known by everyone else and got drawn into conversations with them rather than with Charlie.

For over a month Charlie was completely by herself until she found that the postman always called at 11 a.m. She made a point of being near the door when he came so she could have a word or two with him, and was disappointed when there was no mail and he didn't turn up. There were many days like that because, to begin with, the only letters arriving at Bluebell Cottage were official forms and advertising matter.

But Dean Williams, the postman, was a chatty man who loved his work, and he was always happy to spend a few minutes talking to Charlie. He didn't know, or care, that she had been on the West End stage and that she was a dancer. He was only interested in talking about her garden, the weather, a little local gossip and that sort of thing.

In that month, Charlie's only other real "contact" was with her milkman. Three times a week she got up very early so she could stand in the kitchen window and get a few seconds of companion-ship by waving to him as he ran down the path to get his morning exercise, stopped to drop off her single bottle of milk, then waved to her before running back to his van waiting in the road. Charlie never found out what his name was.

Those two apart, Charlie was alone. Apart from short chats to Dean, she didn't have anyone to talk to, and when she drew the curtains in the evenings she felt completely isolated from the whole world. When she went to bed, she alwa ys pulled the bedroom curtains back for a last look out and it always hit her that there was complete darkness outside—an unwelcome black night with no street or house lights to be seen. When she turned the lights out, there was only that darkness, a deep impenetrable non-life.

Despite that, she didn't sleep well. Charlie would push herself into the mattress, pull the duvet tight round her, and lie with eyes open in the womb of her bed until exhaustion finally took over her body and her mind.

It was never a deep sleep, and she would wake up early in the morning and it was still as if the darkness had got into her mind and being. She hated the thought of getting up and facing the world, and more often than not she was reluctant to get out of bed—she felt safe there and remote from reality.

During the day she was physically conscious of the loneliness of the village, and she started to think that despite the beauty of the countryside there was an ugliness about the whole human race. She felt as if, a cliche, she was in a deep hole in a dark tunnel from which she could not escape. She was, as doctors or nurses would have told her, suffering a growing form of medical depression.

Without anyone to talk to, Charlie thought several times of phoning friends in London, but they were all dancers or other show people and she knew they would be busy at rehearsals or on stage.

They were her past anyway.

She did try watching television to pass the afternoons, but there were only game shows where she invariably answered more than the

contestants or annoying cookery programmes where she devout-
ly wished at least one of the cooks—or chefs as they liked to call
themselves—would say some dish tasted horrible or burn the pan.z

She was lonely.

In a mood of near despair, Charlie tried a day trip to London.
She took the train to Waterloo, then the underground to Piccadilly
Circus. It only took her four minutes on the Bakerloo Line, but the
confinement made her feel quite frightened and hemmed in.

sShe emerged into a grey, dreary London and almost instinctively, without thinking, followed the same route she used to walk
to work, up a Shaftesbury Avenue now empty of tourists, past the
theatre where she once danced and now with another show called
*Twilight Dancing,* starring someone called Jack Silver; she had no
feeling, no emotion, no regret. She knew she did not belong there
now. It was all "might have been".

Charlie carried on walking, then turned right into Endell Street
and then through to Covent Garden, where she found a seat at a
French patisserie. Over a coffee and a sinful cream cake, she watched
the busy throng rushing around speaking on mobile phones. No
one was talking to anyone else. It was all hustle and bustle, and she
couldn't help thinking of Bluebell Cottage. After three-quarters of
an hour—with another coffee and another creamy cake—she stood
up, got a taxi, and went back to Waterloo, and home.

London was a big disappointment for Charlie. She did not feel
part of it anymore, and Theatreland was simply a place where things
might have been.

She realised she had to become part of a quiet country community and determined that no matter how long it took, she would make more effort to fit in with the village and the villagers.

That was easier said than done, and it took time because Charlie had no way of meeting her neighbours. She didn't want to just knock on doors and introduce herself, so she went out for walks, often in the park that stood opposite Bluebell Cottage beside the working men's club. They were lonely walks, because inevitably as she walked around there was no one else in sight, not even by the children's play area in one corner. Sometimes she would try out the roundabout or the swings in that area, but mostly she sat on a seat in a corner or on the grass.

But she was always alone except for the birds flying round, in and out of the trees—the only "conversation" for her was the cawing of the crows or the tweets and chirps of the other unknown birds.

She bought herself a cheap small second-hand car, and in the days and weeks that followed, she went for long, lone drives around the local countryside and visited all the scenic pleasure sites of the area.

Looking out of the windows of her house or while out on her drives, she could see all the insects and birds busy, busy, busy. The animals. The abundance of nature. Her neighbours. Life went on around her tirelessly, and Charlie watched it all but did not feel a part of it.

She tried going for occasional long cross-country walks, but her legs hurt too much for her to go very far, and so eventually she bought herself an exercise bike for the times she did not feel like driving, but the bike was very much second choice. Without thinking, Charlie saw everything that was happening around her but didn't really join in—normally her depression meant she could not be bothered.

One day, mooching listlessly about the house, she "discovered" the diamond bracelet Dane had given her on their ostentatiously romantic date in Paris. It had been put away in a drawer with some other items, still in its velvet case and unworn. When she found it again Charlie looked at it and realised that as beautiful as it was, neither it nor Dane meant anything to her now.

As the initial fervour of the house died down and she looked for something else to do, she tried to get interested in the garden, although bending over the plants hurt her leg more than it should. Then she got the bracelet out again and sold it for quite a substantial sum without a pang of nostalgia.

As the weather improved she returned to her daily drives, and they began to take up many hours in her day, but apart from that she slept, she woke, she ate. She did housework, went shopping and joked with the shelf packers in the nearby supermarket. Sometimes she read a book or a newspaper, or watched TV. But nothing seemed to affect her—she was very lonely, and for a while her life consisted of just existing.

She did speak to her neighbours when she saw them, but they were fleeting moments. One, in particular, annoyed her. Every time Charlie said something, she would repeat it.

"Nice and sunny today."

"Sunny, yes."

"The flowers are nice at this time of year."

"Flowers, yes."

Without thinking, Charlie saw everything that was happening around her, either from the windows of her house or while out on her drives. All the insects and birds. The animals. The abundance of nature. Her neighbours. Life went on around her tirelessly, and Charlie watched it all but did not feel a part of it.

Depression was always somewhere around her, and things began to go from bad to worse. Then one day she was in her local super-market when a stranger walked up to her, looking at her in a funny way. Charlie tried to ignore it.

"Sorry to bother you, but I was a great admirer of you and your shows. I heard about your illness..." said the woman, and when Charlie muttered a quiet thanks, she went on to show real sympathy. "I loved your dancing. Such lovely music..."

It cheered Charlie up for a while.

To counter that meeting though, back in the same shop a couple of weeks later, another middle-aged woman lined up behind her in the checkout queue.

"Didn't you used to be...?" she asked, tailing off as if she couldn't quite remember the name.

Charlie nodded and switched off, then it was her turn to pay and she hurried off feeling bad.

When people did recognise her, their reaction was like that. It was variable, and didn't really matter to her. Or so she thought. But after a while, it hit her that there was no reason for people to know her now. She realised that she was only looking at her past—a past that now seemed a long way away.

Charlie made herself think of the present, of her position after her illness. She missed dancing tremendously, and having to give it up—albeit temporarily, she still hoped—was hard. She missed the delight of performing to music and she missed the sheer glamour and fizz of curtain up. It was better than being ill, she reasoned, but she still had an ache for her life on stage.

But despite that, she still refused to have anything to do with dancing or the theatre, although she did get a few offers through Aaron for her to return to work. She was dispirited in an unaccountable way and could not control her feelings. On the one hand, she still loved the idea of dancing in front of an audience. On the other, she hated the discomfort in her feet and the inability to walk without hurt.

One day, feeling particularly low and trying to rid herself of thoughts about dancing, she even threw out her collection of old Hollywood musical videos, including all the Astaire pictures. She remembered telling film producer Batty Thomas that her favourite scene was the Astaire–Charisse "Dancing in the Dark", and she pondered whether or not to keep just that one, eventually throwing it away with all the others.

But the feeling didn't last. The depression began to lessen, and in an effort to snap out of it completely, she rang Danny for a chat, but she was told he was "in the provinces" trying out a new show. She tried to ring Babs instead. This time she got an answering machine.

Although she rarely thought of it, the illness still hovered in the recesses of her imagination. Every lasting ache or new pain immediately brought thoughts that the cancer had returned. She tried to put the idea out of her mind, but it was there.

By coincidence, a few days after her futile call to Danny, she was feeling quite down when he rang her from her local railway station and asked her to pick him up.

"Harry asked me how you were getting on, so I thought I'd drop in for a cup of tea to find out," he said when she did.

Charlie knew he was covering his own unusual shyness.

As they left the station, a car carved them up, but Charlie caught up at the next traffic lights.

Danny leant out of the window. "They make that model with signals now," he shouted.

It was typical of Danny, thought Charlie, and once again it was a small thing that cheered her up. Then further along on the drive back to her house, she took him down some narrow country lanes with fields showing through the thick hedges on either side.

"Where are all the buses? And the taxis?" asked Danny.

"Buses? We don't have any of that kind of thing round here," replied Charlie. "Haven't you ever been in the wilds of the countryside before?"

"Oo-argh, oo-argh. Just once when I were just a wee calf of a lad. I was born in deepest Dorset, y'know. We only had wild horses down there. I'm a townie now. Thought you were too."

"Not me," answered Charlie. "I'm a real country bumpkin."

They drove on, and Danny seemed to relax as he looked at the thick yellow fields on either side of the lane.

"What's that? In that field?" he asked eventually.

"Corn. It's for my breakfast flakes," smiled Charlie.

"Oh," replied the writer. "We only grew bracken amongst all the rocks where I came from. Where are the Coco Pops fields for my breakfast then?"

They drove on, Danny looking out of his side window. "What are those?" he asked eventually.

"Lambs."

"Lambs... Oh yeah." He opened the window and shouted out, "I had your brother for lunch!"

He was quiet again for a while after that, but then he shifted somewhat awkwardly in his seat. "Was it really bad?" he eventually asked Charlie softly, without looking at her.

Knowing that Danny could, and often did, produce off-the-cuff lyrics on virtually any subject, she told him, "I don't think even you could write about it." She glanced a smile at him in the passenger seat.

Danny didn't reply, still didn't look across at the girl.

Further along he did look across. "So, where are all the people?" he asked. "Out picking all their country produce, I suppose. Or at the village market."

"No," Charlie told him. "We don't have shops or markets out here in the wilds of the countryside. The supermarkets in the towns have killed them all off, and we have to go to them for our victuals. That's where all the people are right now. Buying up the same potatoes and carrots they all grow in the fields. Apart from those left out here in the wilderness growing your Coco Pops on the farms."

As they neared her house, the roads widened a little, and along one side there were huge houses in enormous grounds. Many had ostentatious stone and iron gateway entrances.

"Just big gates and long drives, no houses!" laughed Charlie.

Danny continued looking out of the window. "Skid row," he said.

A little further on, they drove through a small village—just five houses to be seen—and Danny looked from side to side at them all before commenting again.

"Hmm. People round here must all be as rich as you, or Aaron," he added, slumping deep in his seat again as if to hide himself.

"Never mind, wait till you get to my village. That's a slice of real England," said Charlie.

They did get to the village and drove through its main street, and as they got to the end Danny sat up again.

"Real England?" he muttered. "Real England? But it doesn't even have an Indian takeaway!"

"But it does have a pub."

"Bet the cider's Belgian, and warm to boot."

They drew in to the gravelled driveway of Charlie's house. There was lawn all the away round, well-kept flower beds, tall hedges, and flowering wisteria covered the side wall.

Danny looked at it. "That's quite colourful," he said. "What's it called?"

"Wisteria—"

Danny automatically and subconsciously interrupted. "Wistful wisteria," he said.

Charlie ignored him. "Yes, it is pretty, but it's a bit of a nuisance," she continued. "It gets in everywhere. Tangles the guttering, ruins the brickwork... it's the real bane of my life."

"Huh? Hysteria amongst the wisteria, eh?"

"Ah, you can't keep a good lyricist down," said Charlie.

"Oh no. Pity there ain't more people who understand that, but I reckon you only have people writing barn dances and country couplets in these 'ere rural parts," said Danny in a mock country voice.

Once in the house, they had a glass of white wine, and after reminiscing for a while, Danny again asked Charlie about her illness, and Charlie gave him a brief run-through of what it was like.

"The actual operation was... well, just what you'd expect from an operation. I didn't know much about it. I was out for the count," she told him. "Then the chemo... well, that wasn't too bad while it lasted. Boring, because you just sit there with wires dripping stuff into you. You don't feel a thing, and I suppose at the back of your mind you know it's doing you good. The trouble is that sometimes, when it's all over, the after effects linger on..."

"That's why they call them after effects," interrupted Danny.

Charlie again ignored him and continued. "That's what they've done with me. I still get these fuzzy fingers and my feet hurt all the time. I just hope it'll go away soon, but the medics don't seem to know. Some don't even seem to care."

Danny listened sympathetically. "What can I say?" he asked when she paused. "You know I'll do anything I can. If there is anything I can do."

Charlie laughed. "Thanks. In that case, you can pour another glass of wine."

Danny poured the drinks, then sat down facing her. "Have you thought about getting back to work when it's all over?" he asked, serious.

Charlie shook her head and looked down at her feet. She shrugged.

"We've got a new show almost ready. Harry and me. It'll be ideal for you," Danny continued. "Well, maybe not the lead, but there's a great support part for a singer. Almost as big. You could do that."

"Is that why you came here today?"

"No. Well, partly," the writer said. "I really did want to see you, see how you were getting on, and on the way down thought it might be a good idea to get you into the show. It would be great for us and it might be good for you."

Charlie thought for just a second. "N-o-o-o-o," she replied eventually. "I don't think I want to consider it. Not at the moment." She didn't know why she said it. It was an instinctive feeling.

For some reason, Danny did not press the point nor try to persuade her. "Well, maybe you could get back to work as a straight actress," he said eventually, slowly and a little lamely.

"I don't think it's an option," insisted Charlie, "I don't think I could be good enough now, and I don't really want to appear on a stage if I'm not dancing."

They finished their drinks, chatted generalities for a while, then Charlie drove Danny back to the station. Both were a little quiet in the car. As they neared the station, Danny broke the silence.

"I don't even like Coco Pops. I only have toast for breakfast," he said.

Overall, the visit did give Charlie a lift, and the thought that she might still be wanted for a show pleased her despite her refusal to accept the offer.

But the feeling didn't last and the depression returned,

Although it was not the reason—and apart from her conversation with Danny, she rarely thought of it—the illness still hovered in the recesses of her imagination. Every lasting ache or new pain immediately brought thoughts that the cancer had returned. She tried to put the idea out of her mind, but it was there.

And she did seem to get lots of different aches and pains. One day she felt as if she had pieces of grit under her soles, the next aching ankles, the next after that a pain in the arm. And so on. Nothing to do with her knee. All, she presumed, the result of her chemo.

But despite all the problems, over the following months the depression eased and she slowly felt her life starting to rebuild. But it was a very different life to one she had known.

# Chapter 22

# VILLAGE LIFE

When she did eventually start meeting people, Charlie found the villagers were a good bunch. She didn't really begin to see more of them until one Thursday afternoon neighbour Linda brought her a cake she'd baked earlier that day.

"I love baking, and as I was at it earlier, I made an extra cake for you," she said. "I hope you like jam sponges."

Charlie invited her in, and they spent a happy hour over cups of tea and chatting. Linda told Charlie about her other immediate neighbours, and after Charlie had said how lonely she was, she promised to introduce them whenever she could.

"Why don't you come across to the club tomorrow night?" she asked, indicating the working men's club opposite with a flick of her thumb. "A lot of us get together there every Friday for a drink and a gossip. About seven. At least, we girls gossip, but I think the men just drink and occasionally tell dirty stories about us."

They both laughed and a friendship was born.

Through Linda, Charlie gradually got to know many of the others living near her. The day after their chat, she walked cross the road in the growing dark to go into the working men's club looking for Linda and Eric, but they were not there. Charlie was greeted in a friendly way by everyone else though, and one unknown man bought her a glass of red wine. Linda and Eric arrived about ten minutes later, and the evening settled down with everyone very friendly.

Charlie thoroughly enjoyed her "night out", but she was still lonely when she retreated behind the closed doors and curtains of Bluebell Cottage. It was still taking her time to adapt to country life. She didn't really know anyone, and although many people nodded to her and said their hellos when she met them in the street, she still felt apart from everyone.

But that first visit to the club was the start of her slow integration into true village life. She joined the club officially—paying her first five pound annual fee by cash over the bar—and slowly began to feel more like a human being as life started to look much rosier.

After a few weeks, Charlie was invited by one of her Friday night friends to attend a meeting of the village WI, but she didn't enjoy it, especially when she realised that many of the ladies there only wanted her to give a talk about her life on the stage. It was the last thing she wanted to do.

Charlie didn't let that deter her, however, and gradually she got to know more of the residents of Tilstead. She willingly got drawn in to the Friday sessions at the club, and after a while decided to try a meal at the Vixen Hunter again. This time many of the regulars, a lot who also drank at the club, recognised her and greeted her as an equal, and after she had given her order to the landlady Gilly Hawkings, she sat at a table in the corner to watch everyone. Gilly came over after a few minutes and stopped by her table to have a bit of a natter.

Gilly, who was from Liverpool and had quite a strong Scouse accent, was especially chatty. "Understand yous used to be in the business," she said. "That's a coincidence, 'cause I always wanted to go on the stage. I went to a drama and music academy in the Pool and trained for a couple of years to be a pro singer." She laughed, a loud roaring laugh. "I really wanted to be a Beatle, and the academy was no place to learn that. Anyways, I just wasn't good enough. S'pose 'cause I spoke real English." She let loose another uproarious laugh.

Charlie briefly wondered how news of her life as a dancer had spread round the village, but she didn't ask. Instead, she chatted happily to Gilly about singing in general, and then for a while about her own life as a dancer. There was nothing too specific, and it passed some pleasant time. Gilly was very friendly, and stayed with Charlie until her meal arrived and she had to go off to help behind the bar.

After the meal, Charlie stayed at her table for a while absorbing the idle nonsense chatter of the pub, and when she finally left to walk home just down the road, she suddenly realised she had been speaking about life on the stage, and for probably the first time hadn't worried about it. It had become something very much from her past—a pleasant past, but now only worth memories.

As she settled down, Friday drinks at the working men's club opposite her house become a regular for Charlie, and largely due to the people she met there, she quickly became a known and liked part of the community.

She met most of her neighbours there, and began getting invitations to their houses for tea or drinks. She became especially friendly with Linda and Eric Cummings, with Linda fairly regularly bringing her cakes she had baked.

Linda also very kindly stared bringing plates of Sunday roast—or rather, she sent them, with Eric acting as her waiter—and as spring began and the weather brightened up, she often invited Charlie in for afternoon tea or glasses of wine, sitting on easy chairs outdoors in her beautifully tended garden.

One afternoon when she was there, Eric came home from the office early and sat with them drinking a cold beer from the fridge. He joined in the chat, then started to gently tease Charlie about Bluebell Cottage.

"You did me out of a sale," he told her, mock seriously. "I had a buyer all ready to move in, then you came along and did me out of a sale. I lost my commission. I reckon you owe me five thousand pounds to make up for it!"

Charlie played up to it, pretending shock and horror. She over-dramatically put a hand to her mouth, started to stammer, then hanging her head replied in a heavily accented West Country lass accent.

"Oh, sir, I be very sorry," she told Eric, "I'd do *anything* to make it up to you. If there be any way..."

Linda was laughing. "Oh, shut up the pair of you. Let's have another drink," she said simply.

It was another happy day for Charlie. Linda and Eric were a happy-go-lucky couple who laughed a lot, very tied up with their own feelings for each other—shown in the little looks and quiet comments that passed between them—but very caring for others at the same time. Charlie liked them both a lot, and not just because they looked after her.

When she went home that evening, for possibly the first time Charlie knew for sure that she was very much now part of the local scene.

From then on, she was seen and acknowledged by many around the village. She made regular trips to the Vixen Hunter pub, not only because Bill Hawkings cooked wonderful, satisfying meals but to have a good old chin wag with Gilly. They often spoke of music and singing, but never dancing, and when Gilly one evening burst into song for no apparent reason Charlie was quite pleasantly surprised.

"You've got a good voice," she told the landlady.

Gilly was obviously pleased. But realistic. "It was all wrong for me to become a pro," she said. "I tried to hit all the notes, and I tried to breathe properly so I could get the words out right. I still hate all these modern girls—all big boobs and a break in their voice when they can't really reach the note. I'm an old-fashioned girl when it comes to singing." She burst out laughing loudly as usual. "But as I told you once—I was no Beatle."

Slowly, Charlie was getting to know, and be part of, the village, but as spring started to turn to summer, she wanted to see more of the countryside around Tilstead and took to daily drives to start exploring the lanes and scenery for miles around. The car came with a map, and using that and various search engines on her phone, she noted some local beauty spots and set out to explore them.

She started with the remembered Newlands Corner in the Surrey Hills. As she pulled into the last vacant space in its crowded car park, she saw why the area had been deemed "an area of outstanding natural beauty". Sitting on the grass below the park, high on the hill, she looked down over the magnificent views of tree- and grass-lined rolling hills, with oak and yew trees providing a home for thousands of birds of varying kinds and colours that swooped and whooped between them.

She recalled rolling down the grass hill with her mother laughing, but the memory was slightly marred as she became upset that so many people littered the ground around her and rather took away the glory of nature, and she felt how selfish they were. It stuck in her mind.

On another day, following her nose on a much longer drive, Charlie took a rough track off a road outside the village of Chiddingfold—a bumpy road that was more of a three-mile farm track. She drove slowly and carefully, trying to steer round the humps and dips in the unmade road, and at one stage had to brake sharply to a halt when a muster of five peacocks crossed in front of her, their long tails down and trailing in the dust. Peacocks! She had never seen them before, yet here they were in the wild.

As she drove on, there were occasional houses, some big, some twee, and then as she steered round one bend, she had to stop the car again to look at a magnificent bush. It was nearly twelve feet high, and about sixteen or so feet across, and it was packed with an almost solid phalanx of beautiful blue flowers. Charlie thought it alluring.

There was a man standing beside a car outside a house just by the bush, and she wound down her window and asked him what the plant was called.

"It's a hydrangea," he told her.

Back home, she discovered that hydrangea can range in colour from pink to lavender, from purple to violet, and then to blue. The image of that particular shrub stayed with her, and a week later she returned for another look. As she saw it again, she tried to remember its name. She couldn't, so when she saw a man on the opposite side of the road, she stopped to ask him.

"I told you last week," he snapped. "It's a hydrangea!"

Charlie apologised. She hadn't recognised him, and drove off. Despite the man's surly manner, it was still a beautiful bush.

Charlie thoroughly enjoyed her drives in the sun, and on another day, she was taken by the tranquil elegance of another beauty spot closer to home: Frensham Great Pond. She loved the peaceful air around the woodland and water, despite the main road that ran along the far side to where she parked. She decided to go into the hotel that stood on one corner of the pond, and sat on the terrace with a cup of tea served in a delicate cup. It was exquisite, and she looked with a relaxed pleasure at the view and the many small sailing boats that drifted over the surface of the water, sails billowing in the slight, but pleasant, breeze.

It was all very pleasant, and after her long start as a loner in the village, Charlie had settled down. She had made friends, and now she arranged for a young girl to come in once a week to clean the house. It was a job she discovered she disliked, and in any case, it gave her another chance to chat over the inevitable cups of tea.

As she didn't know anything about gardening either, she also got a man to come in to do that, arranging for him to visit fortnightly in the spring and summer and monthly during the winter. Charlie let the gardener, Tom, do what he wanted in the garden, but when he was there, she would wander round the garden asking him what the various plants, flowers and trees were. She loved a huge drooping willow at the back, and was particularly delighted when Tom pointed to a colourful bunched up plant and said it was a small hydrangea. It was much smaller than the one she'd seen on her drive, but it was just as pretty. And it was hers.

Life drifted on, and as Charlie got into the way of things in her new life, she forgot her time in the theatre. Her mind just switched off, and she knew in her mind that she had no regrets.

# Chapter 23

# SETTLING IN

The cancer seemed to be in remission, show business seemed a thing of the past, and Dane was dead (figuratively). Charlie realised that when she read without any emotion at all that he had got engaged to his co-star in a Hollywood musical that was being filmed.

If there was any problem, it was that the after effects of the chemotherapy were proving to be worse than the actual original trouble with her knee. She completed the regular six-monthly scans and checks with Beth Whitehead, the specialist nurse consultant who was part of Dr Hacker's department, without trouble, until at the end of the third year she was told that the checks would be put back to a twelve-monthly interval until the final examination after five years.

She slowly found other topics to talk about, something that seemed to take a dreadfully long time to do. Despite everyone assuring her in the first couple of months that it was obvious she would talk about "the problem", in her own mind Charlie felt that she overdid it.

Although she was settling down in Tilstead, Charlie still sometimes felt as if her life was at a dead end. She had more or less recuperated physically, but she still found herself filling her days "recreating" the local drives time after time, although she had to wear gloves when holding the steering wheel because of the numb feeling in her hands. She hated other drivers who turned or veered off course without giving signals, and one day she had to pull to the side of the road because of the tears in her eyes after a car had suddenly veered left and was halfway round the corner before its brake and signal lights came on. Charlie had to brake violently to avoid running into the back of the car. Quite apart from the bruised feelings, the sudden physical action had made her leg hurt quite a bit as well.

Most times though, she could converse and behave quite happily. Back to normal. Or so it seemed.

She still had good days and bad, but one day, while out for another of her solitary drives, the woods on either side of the road suddenly seemed clearer than usual. Their trees were tall, erect, age-old. Eternal, thought Charlie. Through her open window, she could hear the wind playing music in the leaves, the branches seemed to be dancing to its rhythm. She smiled, and mentally danced with them.

*They'll be here dancing long after I'm gone*, she thought, yet despite that she knew that she herself could not dance, not yet anyway. *Why can't we be like the trees? Why can't I be like them?*

Things like that caused a sadness in her mood. It was not exactly a medical depression, more a general loneliness. Despite her mainly friendly neighbours and the fact that she could manage to fill most of her days with irrelevancies, Charlie was still lonely, and on an impulse, she rang Marguerite and invited her for a week. Marguerite's filming was over and her show had closed, and she agreed, so two weeks later Charlie met her at the station and drove her home. All the way, Marguerite gushed about the scenery, the "quaintness" of the countryside.

They drove past what Charlie called "the lake that's higher than the road" and she pointed it out to Marguerite.

"Merely an optical illusion," said her friend. "Geddit? Mere... like a lake."

Charlie thought how like songwriter Danny she was being. "You're being obscure, just like Danny," she replied.

"Well, I have been seeing him, just occasionally. It must have stuck."

Charlie shot her a glance. "D'you mean...?"

"No, no. Nothing like that. Just a couple of times. Just a drink now and then. Between auditions."

She seemed reluctant to talk about it, but Charlie was pleased that her two best friends seemed to be getting on well.

After just a couple of days though, both began to hate the visit. Charlie became frustrated because Marguerite kept talking about the show and film she had just completed and about her future theatrical plans. It was obvious that Marguerite, despite anything she said to please Charlie, really hated the quiet of the country.

Outwardly, they appeared to get on just as well as always, but both began inwardly counting down the days to the end of the week.

One day, after they had driven to the local supermarket to get something for an evening meal, Charlie began raging about some of the things that upset her: at other shoppers who looked at the magazines on a rack by the checkout as they waited their turn, then chattered to the cashier, and finally when it was all done, held up the other shoppers as they rummaged amongst their shopping bags for handbags, looked for purses, and only then found a credit or debit card. Standing in line behind them, it made Charlie's leg ache, she complained, and she wondered why they had not got the card out while they were waiting.

Marguerite listened, but was unmoved. "You're getting to be like a grumpy old lady," she said, and she was only half joking.

Charlie quietly understood that her friend was simply telling the truth, and after Marguerite had gone home, she realised she was becoming a settled, small village bumpkin. But the serenity of the countryside helped her try to get her mind and body together and come alive again.

An over-riding feeling of apathy began to depress her again. She suddenly had no real interest in village life around her, a lack of motivation and an emotional detachment.

She realised she might never dance again, ever—it was now more than a possibility—but despite that, her longing for rhythmic move-ment began to return slowly. She missed her days on stage. She longed to dance, itched to perform to music as she used to.

She tried to dance round in the privacy of the living room of her house with the radio on, but she very quickly had to stop that because it was too uncomfortable. And as her feelings for the theatre returned, she tried to wipe them from her mind altogether, although they still remained, niggling away.

Moments of depression like that, however, were usually countered by Charlie's growing determination not to let her illness affect her and her recovery. By now she was slim and fit, and her hair had fully regrown; she now wore it layered, fashionably shoulder length. Her life was more or less getting back to some form of normality.

Reading a magazine in the hairdresser one day, she noticed that Dane's engagement in Hollywood had been called off. She didn't bother reading the whole article to find the reason because it had no emotional effect on her, and later she realised that was another step forwards. She shrugged her shoulders metaphorically.

Some days were still worse than others physically though, and then she just literally gritted her teeth, bit her bottom lip, and tried to go for short walks. Her feet and ankles still hurt, so she often used the exercise bike instead.

She still drove round the countryside more than she walked—it was easier—but on the better days she did manage to stroll short distances through the woods on the hills near her house or at nearby Newlands Corner. She loved it there, high in the hills, and thought how poetic it was. You could hear the silence of the scenery above the noise—the background chatter, an aeroplane, a mower in the distance—but above it all, you could hear the silence.

She often stopped to watch lambs gambolling near their mothers, or cows contentedly standing or sitting in groups depending on whether it was wet or dry, or horses serenely grazing or nuzzling up to each other nose to neck.

She was fascinated by one tree—a tree again—that had fallen or been blown over at some time and now lay on its side with its roots curling round and back into the earth, but the strange thing was that its branches had grown out and upwards like tree trunks themselves, all reaching for the sunlight.

One day, she saw and exchanged smiles with an old resident walking along briskly, and remembered that when she had first arrived in the village the woman had ridden her horse with her pet dog on the saddle in front of her. She was surprisingly glad that the old lady still seemed to recognise her.

"I haven't seen you for a long time," said the old lady.

"Oh, I've been here, but I've been very busy lately. It's all settling down now though," replied Charlie.

"Good to see you. How's your mother?"

Charlie ignored that. "Good to see you still getting around," she said instead.

"Yes, well, the horse died. Then the dog. It's all a bit lonely now."

Charlie thought she might go visiting some time. But instead, she had withdrawn into herself to quite an extent, and apart from occasional meetings with neighbours, the old lady or shopkeepers, she rarely saw anyone these days. She became quite reclusive, and only infrequently did she feel the need for company. Although she never seemed to do very much, the days passed quickly.

One of her greatest "friends" was a chirpy little robin—one of the many birds who nested in the high hedges around her house—who turned up every morning to sit on her windowsill with his head cocked to one side to say "hello". He had been around for three years, and Charlie would stand on her side of the glass chatting to him, and the robin looked as if he understood her.

Occasionally, very occasionally, she would climb to the top of a nearby knoll and look over the majestic scenery disappearing into the distance in misty, hilly layers. From one, there was always a thin plume of white smoke climbing straight into the sky from a house or farm she could never quite see.

On her frequent long drives, she enjoyed the countryside and the tall woods and forests of the Surrey Hills, while across the boundary into Hampshire about a mile from her home, there would be the huge farm fields with their soldierly lines of growing crops alternating with the regimented lines of ploughed furrows.

While cruising along, she would see the birds soaring over her, riding the wind, flying free. It had been the same for her when she was dancing. She had felt free then, flying free as the birds.

She would see the horses, cows and sheep in the fields, and the small wild animals nipping into the bushes at the side of the road. Rabbits, hares, sometimes foxes. Pairs of partridges standing in the middle of the road staring stupidly at her car and having to be shooed away with the hooter.

She remembered that when she used to go for drives with her mother, she had once asked whether the cows and sheep had longer legs on one side so they could stand upright on the sides of the hills. Her mother had laughed, and Charlie smiled at the recollection.

She loved reading the house names as she drove past—those that showed a vague touch of local history like the Old Oast House or the Old Village Store; the less obvious Muriel's Cottage—who, she wondered, was Muriel?—or Hankin's Folly. There was Five Oaks, which only had one oak tree in its sumptuous garden, and Long View—the obvious, and therefore boring—Dunromin and Mon Repos. Vale Mansion only had a huge iron gate between massive brick pillars leading to a long drive—but no house that she could see—and there were innumerable "cottages" which were in fact five-bedroom mansions with enormous grounds.

Some names were, to her mind, just plain funny: Wyffesnaym, Penn Uri Cottage. She had to read some of those out loud to get a smile. And she thought she was very rude when she smiled at a house called Peewee!

There were two she loved in particular, both very old. One was Elizabethan with really high chimneys, pillared porches and leaded windows, and an enormous garden behind a huge hedge, and she remembered, sadly, that her mother said tall Elizabethan chimneys were something to do with wealth taxes. The other house was a slightly more recent build, but with an immaculate, tiered garden that was obviously tended with love. Both had huge, imposing frontages, and she would slow down when driving past as she adored looking at them both.

And then there was Hollow Oak House just up the road. She loved it, and still could not walk or drive past it without recalling that, as a six-year-old, she had thought that fairies lived inside the tree. She still wondered if they did, but she did not have the nerve to knock on the door and ask.

She loved the small villages with the serenity they wore with ease, the old churches with their ancient gravestones giving an air of eternity. But as she drove through them, she often wondered why they all had signs exhorting people to "Please drive carefully through our village". Did that mean you could drive recklessly when you reached the end?

Then soon it was winter and the snow fell heavily. Really heavily. The evocative smell of neighbours' burning log fires would come to her through the window of her house, and once again her memory reminded her of days with her mother driving around seeing the snow on the hills and in the woods. But within a couple of days, the sides of the road outside her house were lined with piles of snow thrown from the wheels of passing cars that had turned black and mucky. It was, she felt, a reflection of her life: all beauty, then horribly dirty.

It did, indeed, sum up her new life. The falling snow of winter, the falling rain of spring, the falling leaves of autumn. Life and the land went on without change, but her own life had changed, and changed a lot.

Then finally she was called in for her final fifth-year scan and appointment with Nurse Whitehead. The scan went off as smoothly as usual, but the week-long wait to get the result seemed to stretch to eternity. Charlie worried, fretted, anguished. Yet on the day of the appointment with the nurse, she dallied, apprehensive, as much as she could without being late.

Everything was fine, and Nurse Whitehead quickly put her at her ease with the news.

"Nothing on the scan and your blood readings are OK. I think we can say goodbye to you now," said the nurse.

As with the oncologist years earlier, Charlie felt she could kiss the older woman. She got a reproving look when she suggested it, but it was a reproving look with a smile on the lips.

"Remember what's happened to you though," Nurse Whitehead went on, "You're over it. You've done the five years, but you're now like the rest of us. You take your chances like all of us."

But Charlie was only aware that everything was fine. She left the hospital feeling marvellous. At last, she was in complete remission. Cured. The cancer was over. Officially.

The euphoric feeling of high elation faded over the next days and weeks, of course. It had been a long journey, but nowhere near as bad as she'd imagined it was going to be all those years back when she had first started the chemo. Five years of her life, but now it was over and she was fine. It was funny, she thought. She had balked at first at the thought of things ever getting back to normal. Now she was almost scared to admit that they were right again, and scared in case they weren't. That a mistake had been made in the final scan.

As the idea settled into her mind though, the fears finally faded and things slowly became more or less all right both mentally and on the fitness front. Her life had become so methodically tied in with the continuing medical treatment that she had been forced to reorganise herself and begin working things out in a very orderly manner.

She still had to take pills, and they were taken very precisely at the same time every day—although she sometimes forgot and was furious with herself—and clothing was put away as soon as it was discarded. It was different to her former way of doing things at home, and her life started working to a very careful pattern, moving her former stage organisation to that of real life. It was, although she didn't realise it, almost like playing a role.

Her depression more or less disappeared, and she now accepted that she would never dance again, although she would not admit it, she still did want to admit it. In bed at night, she realised her life was going nowhere.

Then one day, she was once again sitting down the hill below the car park at Newlands Corner, a happy smile on her face as she leant back on her elbows breathing deeply and enjoying the heavy sunshine as she watched old couples walking together slowly down the hill and even slower on the way back up and harassed young mums trying to keep their ultra-energetic young children from running into them. For some reason, she noticed a young man walking rather briskly towards her swinging his arms and leading a dog on a leash. As she watched, she realised that what had caught her attention was the way he walked, and as he got closer, she studied him until she realised he had an artificial leg and was forcing himself to walk normally.

When he paused near her, Charlie stood and began speaking to him. He told her he was a soldier who had lost one leg entirely and needed a new knee in the other after a mine blast in action overseas, and he said he was still learning to walk "normally" again.

"I want to march on my company's medal parade in a month," he told her. "And you can bet that when I do, no one will particularly notice me."

Charlie was struck by his determination. It immediately made her equally determined to completely get over what she suddenly regarded as her own "minor inconvenience".

# Chapter 24

# DANCING AT THE FETE

Life settled back to a near normal, and Charlie started going back to the working men's club opposite Bluebell Cottage again. Friday evenings were a big social time when everyone in the village joined in, and she went there regularly every week and was accepted,

There was something of a surprise when she paid her usual trip to the club one Friday though. On that particular day, she got a shock with a brief and unexpected reminder of her former existence. As usual, she was sitting on a high stool at the bar waiting for her friends to come in when a stranger came over to her.

"Didn't I see you dancing some time?" he asked. "In the West End? You're..." He paused, trying to think of her name.

Charlie delayed a moment. "Yes, I was dancer," she finally said, "But that was a long time ago."

The man went red in the face and neck. "Oh, I'm sorry. I didn't mean to intrude."

"Don't worry about it," replied Charlie, seeing Linda coming through the door. "It's just that I'm a different person now."

She forgot about the incident, but when she got home a couple of hours later, she reflected that she had been right. She *was* a different person. Show business had no part in her life now.

Things were different, and she found country loneliness a complete contrast to the way she had felt in London. There were less people around, yet she felt more part of a group. It was strange. Instead of having people barging across you or bumping into you, now it was wild animals in the fields who scurried out of your way. It was a much more relaxed way of living, and she was enjoying it all.

Not one of the village regulars, apart from Gilly Hawkings occasionally, seemed to care two hoots about her career on the stage, and she could wander round and see what made the parts of the village she didn't know tick.

There was, for instance, the annual Tilstead Village Show. Although she was not quite ready to take an active part in the show, which took place in the park behind the club and opposite her house, she looked forward to the day and was determined to visit it.

The show was held on a Saturday afternoon, and in the two days before it started, a large marquee and several smaller tents were set up to hold the various exhibits and the village life contests. On the day itself, cars started parking in the road outside Bluebell Cottage, and before she left the house, Charlie heard sounds of a large crowd making its way to the show.

When she joined them, the sun had risen high and the day was hot, although the many trees round the edges of the park gave a certain amount of shade. Charlie walked round the field chatting to many of the people she recognised, and who recognised her, and took a keen interest in the many exhibits—the displays of cake making, baking, arts and crafts, and photography amongst them. She enjoyed looking at the displays in the huge exhibition tent, especially the horticultural array of homegrown vegetables and the huge bouquets of beautiful flowers in a myriad of shining bright colours. There was a small village history stand too.

She watched a parade of groomed dogs of assorted breeds, all prettied and adorned to an extraordinary level, and then a display by mainly elderly men manoeuvring their prim horses and carts through a series of obstacles. She thought many of the home art paintings by some of the villagers showed real talent.

There were also fun side shows, such as pelting a young lad in stocks, tossing a hoop—she had six goes and missed the pole every time—and many others.

Everything she saw delighted her as she wandered around, chatting at length to the people she knew and had met, and to others she had never seen before. It was all as she had imagined life would be like in the quieter life of a country village.

It was well into the afternoon before she began to feel tired, in part by the unexpected simple excitement round her but mainly by having a hot sun beating down on her uncovered head, and she started to make her way home.

Before she left though, she heard an announcement that made her wander to a large square ring to watch a display of country dancing. She didn't know an awful lot about this kind of dance, so she listened intently as the announcer explained that it was a form of social folk dancing dating back many centuries, performed by a fixed set of steps.

She loved it when the dancers stepped into the ring dressed in traditional costume to form two long lines. They paired off and linked arms, then skipped round in a circle to face the original way before an instructor called out the fixed steps for them as they traditionally moved along the lines followed by the next couple. It was all set in stone, but informal, and the music set up a rhythm that captured the minds of the onlookers.

As she watched, Charlie's feet started to automatically carve out the moves, her left foot starting to track the dancers in the ring, then both feet and her body. It was without thought, just her basic inbuilt love of dancing, and after a few moments, she found she was replicating the moves at the side of the ring. Another girl standing next to her joined in and although they didn't know each other, they did their own country dance arm in arm together.

The particular song ended and the two girls applauded both the dancers and themselves, laughing happily. Charlie bowed low to her partner, and the dancing of the troupe started again to a new song.

Charlie's thoughts surprised her as she somehow knew that despite her little dance, she no longer had any thoughts of show biz. She still subconsciously missed dancing, but she no longer craved footlights and a stage.

As the dancing continued, she told herself that she should probably look up local dance groups and maybe join one of them.

After half an hour more of the dance exhibition, Charlie moved away and went home. She arrived and slumped on the sofa with her feet resting on a low coffee table in front of her. She realised there was a slight twinge in the knee she had hurt some time before. The first time she had felt it for months.

It was so bad that she decided that, although she obviously still loved dancing, she would give the formal evening dance in the fete's main marquee a miss, and it was lucky she did, because next morning her knee was heavily swollen. It puzzled Charlie because she didn't think she had put too much pressure on her knee, but something was obviously wrong and she wondered if she should go see a doctor. She was a little scared of doing so, and a few days rest—hardly going out—allowed the knee to settle and return to normal. After that, it didn't hurt at all.

Two weeks after the fete, Charlie received a letter from an ageing aunt, forwarded from her London address and telling her that "the authorities" were trying to force her into a care home because of growing dementia.

*I've been managing to care for myself at home for a while, but I can't manage anymore,* she wrote. *I need looking after, and I thought you might want to do that.*

Charlie didn't feel any emotion when she read the letter. Since the death of her parents, she had hardly had any contact with her family, and she felt this request out of nowhere was highly selfish. She decided there was no way she could now return to her family.

She sent a brief note turning down the suggestion and carried on with her life without looking back.

The trouble was that, after the letter and her reply, for a while Charlie became a bit morose again, withdrawn and just as lonely as before. She drifted, and was quite happy when she drew the curtains in the evening, shutting out what she regarded as a cruel world outside. It was a dark time again, but after a couple of weeks the new-found optimism over her developing life in Tilstead returned, and life settled down.

Once again Charlie found enjoyment in all manner of things. It was getting towards summer, and the scenery all round her was delightful. She enjoyed the bright flowers in her garden, and the greens and browns of the trees lining the roads, lanes and hills, and the colourful fields of yellow nearby.

People around the village were talking to her, even the checkout girls in her local supermarket smiled and asked her how she was. It was much more acceptable, much better than the bleak loneliness of before, although there was still something niggling in her mind. Something she felt was missing in her life. Try as she might, she couldn't think what it was, what it might be.

# Chapter 25

# ALAN

Life plodded on at a slow country pace, and once again Charlie slotted into a round of teas with neighbours and friends, meals and chats with Gilly Hawkings at the Vixen Hunter, and drinks at the club. It was, once again, quiet, settled, and routine, and she enjoyed it.

The talks with Gilly especially pleased her. Although her theatre life was over, Charlie still enjoyed song and dance and would often talk to her landlady friend about them. Gilly had strong views on both singers and dancers and expressed them vividly. Charlie usually disagreed—not necessarily because she believed one was better than the other. She just loved to "discuss".

Both women loved the talk and the half-hearted disagreements, and they laughed a lot about it all.

Laughing proved good news in helping Charlie overcome any remaining feelings of seclusion and despair, and that mood was further enhanced one day when she met neighbour Eric as he was arriving home.

"Got some valuations in today," he paused to tell her. "Reckon your house has practically doubled in price since you've been here."

Charlie felt better than she had for a long time. But if solitude was no longer a real problem, there was still that unsettling feeling that something was missing from her life.

Meeting friends and neighbours in the working men's club on Friday evenings was still Charlie's main socialising event of the week. Every time she went she met new people, and one evening Eric introduced a young-looking man called Alan Collins. He had a happy face, with a friendly smile that lit it up. His blue eyes were bounded by dark eyebrows, strangely at odds with his light blonde hair.

Alan was casually dressed and casual in nature. He chatted easily to Charlie, using an occasional double meaning remark. He was cheeky, but amusing and likeable, she thought. When she finally left to go home, Alan solemnly took her right hand, bowed over it, and kissed it as a goodbye.

Back home, Charlie thought about Alan. He was nice, good-looking and fun. The thought came back a couple of times during the ensuing week, and by Friday Charlie went to the club a little later than usual, kind of daring fate. And there he was, the only customer talking to Sylvia, the young girl serving behind the bar. As Charlie entered, he looked round, smiled at her, and turned back to the bar.

"A glass of whatever missy wants," he said.

When Charlie got level, a glass of red wine was already on the bar.

"Thank you," she said demurely.

It was a good start to the evening.

It got better from Charlie's point of view. There were few other customers, and Charlie stayed late. Alan was able to spend almost all of the evening with her, refusing to let her buy any drinks and joking, teasing and flirting in a way that amused her. The flirtations were too obvious to be taken seriously, but at the same time Charlie sensed that Alan could be quite serious about his mentions of further meetings.

She wondered about a romance, but laughed at herself for thinking like a naive romantic idiot in a musical. Then Alan did invite her out.

"I hope you don't mind me asking... I've been nerving myself to do it. But there's a good film on at the local cinema," he said. "It's a musical and got good reviews..."

Charlie thought he sounded just as she had felt—a soppy romantic—but before she could answer he went on.

"You do like musicals, don't you?"

He looked quite alarmed, but Charlie laughed and told him that she had once been a professional dancer.

"Of course I love musicals, any kind," she said. "I'd love to see it."

They fixed a date for the following week, and then ignored it for the rest of the evening. It was a happy night, but before she left Alan reminded Charlie.

"I'll meet you here at seven on Tuesday," he told her. "Maybe have a snack before."

Charlie looked forward to the date, and sharp on time the following Tuesday she went across to the club. She had carefully thought of and chosen a flared dark blue skirt with a bright, sparkly blouse and a blue choker round her neck. Thinking about it beforehand, she had tried to remember how tall Alan was, and selected medium-high thin heeled black shoes.

Alan was waiting outside the club in his usual casual outfit, standing beside a family-sized silver car. As Charlie walked across, he opened the passenger door for her and she got in, then he drove them the four miles to the Metro cinema. He asked if she wanted to be dropped at the door, but she said she would stay with him as he went to the car park.

Inside, she found he had already booked ultra-comfortable premium seats, and as they started to make their way inside, he asked her to wait a moment. She stood beside an attendant as he hurried back to the foyer, reappearing a couple of moments later with two huge tubs of popcorn.

"Got to do it properly on a first date," he joked with a happy smile on his lips. "Can't have you thinking I'm a cheapskate."

The film was lively and good, but it finished earlier than they both expected, and when it was over Alan invited Charlie to a nearby Italian restaurant for a "quick bite of supper". Over pizzas he asked about her dancing, and Charlie explained about her training and her injury, and about her venture into a West End show, playing down the fact she had starred in the shows and a film, and not telling him about the cancer. She didn't mind talking about her theatrical career for a change, and things went well.

In turn, Charlie asked Alan what he did for a living. With a hint of a blush and a slight smile, he told her he was a lecturer at a small Midlands university specialising in film, media studies—and dance! He was currently on a six-month sabbatical.

Charlie thought it quite hilarious. "Why didn't you tell me before I rabbited on?" she laughed. "It's really very naughty of you."

Alan explained that he had been told she'd been on the stage but wanted to find out more to get the real story, only partly to see if it matched up to his lectures on dancers.

"But please don't think that's the only reason I asked you out," he went on, his face going a little red again. "I'm fascinated by dancers, but I'm far more interested in people. With…" he stammered to a stop.

Charlie waved him down. "Oh, stop it," she replied. "It doesn't worry me at all. In fact, I think I'm rather flattered, and you're the first person I've told about my show biz past."

Alan was calmed, and went on to tell Charlie he had been raised in the South East, where his father taught piano and his mother was in a choir that broadcast quite frequently. Music had been his upbringing, but he had never liked playing an instrument or singing and had always been a dance nut. He always saw musical films, and because his mother and father were both avid fans, he had always particularly loved Fred Astaire and Ginger Rogers.

"I think we must disagree on that. She wasn't his best partner," she said. "But not this evening. It would ruin a nice time."

Charlie enjoyed the evening, and when Alan drove her home and got out to open the door to let her out of the car, she leant forwards and gave him a sisterly kiss on the lips.

"I've enjoyed tonight," she told him. "Even the bit where you fooled me into revealing all my secrets of life in the wicked theatre!" She smiled at him.

Alan didn't say a word as he let Charlie walk up the short driveway to her house. As she unlocked the door and turned to wave goodbye, he called out.

"I'll see you over the road on Friday," he said. "We'll fix another da—outing."

The following Friday came, and the next and the next. Alan and Charlie not only met at the club, they went out frequently, twice or three times a week. They were getting very involved in each other, and Charlie's thoughts were very much along romantic lines.

They went to pubs, back to the cinema—it was a gloomy melodrama and they walked out halfway through—for meals in cheap burger bars or fairly high-priced restaurants. And they talked.

More often than not it was about music or dancing, although they spoke of many other things. When dancing was mentioned, their differences over Fred Astaire and his partners came up frequently, and they had some wonderfully friendly wrangles about the various pairing. Alan insisted that Ginger Rogers was Astaire's best partner.

"Just look at the popularity of their films together," he repeated over and over.

Charlie stood up for Cyd Charisse or Eleanor Powell. She said she didn't rate Rogers as a solo dancer especially, although she did admit that her partnership with Astaire had certainly captured the public imagination of the time.

"But Astaire was better with Cyd Charisse," she insisted. "Their 'Dancing in the Dark' scene has got to be one of the most romantic dances ever filmed."

And she would back up her anti-Rogers argument by saying that when Astaire danced his tap routine to "Begin the Beguine" with Eleanor Powell, it was far better than anything he did with Ginger.

"That was sheer perfection," she insisted. "It was one of the greatest dances of all time. Powell was probably the only girl who ever out-danced Astaire. He admitted it."

Their dance conversations were not only limited to Fred Astaire though. They chatted about the great choreographers, about the major ballet stars of the world, and about modern gyrating which both described as "gymnastics" rather than dance. They spoke, rarely, about world matters, and about furniture, houses and the like. But it was largely about music and dance.

Charlie liked their talks. Dancing was in her blood, and talking about it easily with Alan bought out her love for it.

But it was not only talking to him that she liked. She enjoyed every moment with Alan, and he seemed to be the same with her. Romance was certainly in the air. They began seeing each other even more often, and Charlie's thoughts were definitely turning towards marriage. There was something about Alan that hit all the right notes for her. Like a good song, the notes were all right and in the right order.

Alan too seemed to have the same feelings. He was attentive, bought Charlie presents, and said all the nice words. It seemed a perfect alliance.

Then suddenly, Alan had to go back to work. He got a letter offering him a one-year university job in Berlin, a job he had been chasing for a long, long time. He felt he could not turn it down, and suddenly he began thinking of lectures and of educational matters, and his whole attitude changed.

Charlie realised it but kept her feelings to herself and had to accept it. In her mind, she began to think that true love was not for her. After all, Alan had never mentioned anything about love or marriage, no words had ever been said. It was all in her own mind, she thought. *Stupid girl. Silly.*

A couple of weeks later, Alan was gone, without a proper farewell. It seemed that one evening he was there with Charlie, the next morning he was gone and Charlie was alone again.

For the first time in a long time, Charlie did not know what to do. At a loss on that first morning, she went out for a walk to try to clear her head, and as she moved through her garden to get to the road, she realised that although he had often been at her house, Alan had never once been in the garden.

She missed Alan but forced herself not to think of him and reluctantly made herself get back into her old rhythm of Friday clubbing, meeting neighbours, and going for drives, and she became reasonably happy with life again. She still welcomed the daily ritual of drawing the curtains around the house to shut out the world, but now she welcomed more the mornings when she opened them again to show her the beauty of burgeoning nature. She lapped it up.

Charlie was resigned to being back on her own, but the feeling that there was still something missing in her life came back, and persisted.

# Chapter 26

# THE SCHOOL SHOW

By chance, the very next day she read in a local paper about a small dance school's annual show to be held in her village hall. She decided to go along to see what it was all about. *Probably just six-year-old girls prancing around to delight their mums and dads*, she thought, and it occurred to her that if it was reasonable, she would try to get involved. It struck her as a possible opportunity to get back into the world of people and dance rather than just thinking nostalgically about dancing. The timing somehow seemed to her as if it had been preplanned.

The show itself was far better than she had imagined. The school was being run by a youngish girl she had often seen around the village, and she had done a very good job training the girls. The pupils ranged from the expected six-year-olds to a very pretty, grown-up-looking teenager, named in the home-printed programme as Zoe Wheeler.

Zoe was coming up to eighteen. She had long auburn hair tied back into a huge ponytail, and she obviously had talent, albeit to Charlie's eye she was not yet quite professional. Her solo won huge applause from the local audience, with one middle-aged man especially shouting, whistling, whooping and calling encouragement.

After the show, there was wine and nibbles, and Charlie introduced herself to Zoe and the man who had been cheering for her. He turned out to be Zoe's father, and he recognised her and enthusiastically told his daughter about Charlie's career as a professional.

"I often saw you on stage, and I went to see your big film at least three times," he boomed enthusiastically.

Zoe was overwhelmed that "such a big star" would bother with her, and at the same time Charlie was surprisingly flattered and delighted that she was still remembered.

Later, Charlie managed to talk to the school's proprietor and found out her name was Felicity Moore. They chatted about the show, and Charlie asked about the school itself.

"I always wanted to be a dancer—a real dancer—but I could never get the break," Felicity told her. "Guess I just wasn't good enough. I couldn't just give it up though, so I started teaching others instead."

She said she had been teaching dance at a local primary school but wanted to branch out and start her own class, and when the opportunity opened up for her to do so, she grabbed it. She had about eight pupils ranging from toddlers to a couple of teenagers.

Her school had been running for about three years, she said, and it turned out that although she had no formal training herself, she had managed to get one or two pupils into a bigger stage school, and one had even passed an exam to a major stage academy in London.

"It's been more of a success than I could ever have hoped for," she went on. "But it's grown, and it's got to the stage now where

I'm beginning to think I probably need help. Someone to advise me on how to take the next step, literally, the next step."

On an impulse, Charlie asked if she could help.

"I wouldn't be able to do much of the dancing, I'm afraid. My knee is a bit wonky and swells when I do any real dancing, but I could show the girls what to do. As you know, I've had a lot of experience and I think I could give you some ideas," she said.

Felicity knew all about Charlie's career, and illness, and accepted without a thought.

"If you could do that, explain things, perhaps I could do the practical work to show it off," she replied, then hurriedly added, "Not so well, of course, but..."

Charlie smiled. "Let's give it a go then, shall we?"

They agreed, and Charlie began work in the village hall a week later.

# Chapter 27

# THE SCHOOL

Felicity Moore was about half an inch shorter than Charlie, with long black hair that reached down almost to her waist. She was slim and athletic, younger by years than Charlie and with an innocent-looking face that normally showed her emotions and made her seem even younger still. Her brown eyes revealed a clear way to her uncomplicated thoughts, and there was nothing insincere showing through.

From the start, she and Charlie got on exceptionally well together. They supplemented each other, their ideas on dancing almost identical and with Felicity able to transfer Charlie's more experienced ideas into practical demonstrations. Charlie was happy. She knew she could not yet perform herself, but working through her partner at the school was the next best thing—an alternative and not the best, but acceptable. She quickly settled into the part.

In the beginning Charlie felt wrong going back to work, mixing with others, the children and their parents, but the work got her over that feeling and fairly quickly things became more or less alright on both the mental and the fitness fronts. Surprisingly, although it shouldn't have, the system of working with Felicity clicked and the pupils of the school loved learning from them both. As word spread locally, more youngsters joined the classes, boys and girls.

Zoe, particularly, bloomed. She had been good to start with, and with the impetus of Charlie's professional background she grew in ability and stature.

Then it was winter, then summer, then winter again, and finally spring. The leaves of the trees in the woods around the village turned from rich green to golden red to brown and then shrivelled to nothing. The flowers and shrubs in Charlie's garden turned from bright colours to gaunt branches, and then back and then back again and yet again in the eternity of nature.

Charlie was feeling better all the time, although she still had the same mixed-up feelings about wanting to dance and not being able to dance. The feelings confused her, but she always managed to put them to one side as she returned to the "normal Surrey life" and her dance school work.

She loved watching the youngsters dance—mostly badly, although always with endeavour and determination—but she never joined in.

Then one evening, after a whole day at the school, she dug out an ancient Gene Kelly CD and listened to it. The music lilted and flowed, and she once again got a strong, almost unbearable, urge to dance herself. Knowing how she had switched off since her illness and trying to rekindle the spirit, she booked to see a musical show at a local theatre to see how it might affect her and how she might react to seeing live dancing again.

She loved it as much as ever and the yearning grew throughout the show: the wish to be on a stage, to sing or dance a solo, to whirl round with her fellow "gypsies", the ensemble numbers, the duets, the singing, the dancing.

Soon, she was working quite a lot with the school, almost daily, giving advice through Felicity and another young dance teacher, Anne, who had been called in to help because the school was growing so fast, partly because news of Charlie's involvement attracted a lot of attention.

"Do I miss dancing?" she frequently asked herself—invariably answering "No" out loud but mentally registering a strong "Yes, of course".

But the tingling in her hands and feet constantly told her it was a no-go. More often than not, her hands felt sticky, and although she knew—by touching her fingers to her face—they were not, she washed her hands virtually every half hour or so. It was a new, unpleasant side effect after the chemo.

The scar on her left knee had healed completely by now, leaving a bulbous jagged run down the whole length of it. She occasionally had icy cold jabs in her ankles—they almost always went away after about five minutes—and she still had mental scars she did not know about so that whenever she had an itch or an ache in her leg, she couldn't help wondering if "the problem" was coming back.

She was still the same weight as before her operation. She looked fit and well, but now there were traces of grey at the sides of her regrown hair. But all she could do, and convinced herself she wanted to do, was carry on working at the school with her old life being recreated by her partner Felicity, by Anne and especially by Zoe.

She still spent a lot of time going on her local drives, and where before she had been ill she had only really read scripts, she was by now an inveterate reader, ordering book after book through her computer. She had large bookcases built by a local craftsman in most rooms, and they filled up rapidly as she devoured both hardback and paperback novels of all kinds. She read all sorts, but not biographies or tittle-tattle reveal-all books normally ghost written for stage or film people.

She still got the show biz paper Variety, and in it she read, again, that Dane was getting married to the leading lady of his Broadway show that weekend. She wondered if she should send a card, but it took only a few moments to decide against it.

Then one day, she was at home when the doorbell rang, and when she answered, there was Aaron, looking embarrassed. She was not surprised—turning up on her doorstep suddenly was a habit he had built up over the years—and she invited him in.

"I just came by to bring you a birthday card," he said, handing over an envelope which seemed to Charlie rather bulky.

She suddenly realised that today was, indeed, her birthday: her thirty-fifth birthday. She was touched that Aaron had remembered, and before opening the card, poured them both a celebratory drink. She sat down, and Aaron put his hand out to stop her picking up the card.

"Open it when I've gone," he said.

Instead, Charlie raised her glass to toast Aaron and he toasted her birthday, then they sat and chatted while he told her what was happening with his latest show.

"Oi, the troubles with my leading lady... nothing like you. You was so easy to work with..." As always, he accented the Jewish accent when he spoke of his production work—and money!

They chatted amiably about nothing in particular, and during the visit Aaron told her that Danny and Marguerite now seemed to be spending a lot of time together.

"Is it a romance?"

Aaron shrugged. "He's writing some lovely love songs..."

After about an hour, Aaron mumbled an excuse and made to leave. Charlie insisted on driving him back to the station.

On the way, going down one of the narrow country lanes, she had to hold back because of a young girl being led on a horse.

"Don't they have cars down here in the wilds?" asked Aaron.

Charlie laughed, and said it was all part of living in the country. She thought that Aaron's comment was very townie—just like Danny and Marguerite had been—but she laughed at the older man.

As they continued towards the station, Charlie told him about her local dance classes, telling him that, although she enjoyed it, she was not getting anywhere near the same pleasure out of it that she'd had when performing in his shows. Aaron was sympathetic, but slightly embarrassed.

At the station, Charlie watched him go on the platform and then went home, thinking first about Danny and Marguerite, then as she returned to the country lanes that she probably had been missing the "bright lights" of London. She went into the house with that thought in her mind, and straight away opened Aaron's birthday card. Inside was a diamond brooch with a tag attached it: "For helping me move to the big time."

A few days later, Marguerite phoned.

"I'm up the duff," she said.

"Is it…?" asked Charlie.

"Oh no, nothing to do with Danny. Just a fella. I thought he was gay, but he wasn't."

"What about Danny? I heard you were seeing him."

"No, he's just a mate. I told him about the baby, and he's been making me laugh to take my mind off it." Marguerite sniggered. "I keep telling him it's not my mind that needs to be anaesthetised, it's my belly. I can't ignore that," she said.

Nothing about her had changed, it seemed, but Charlie felt particularly alone after getting the news.

# Chapter 28

# GEOFFREY

It was just as well then that Charlie returned to the dance school the next day. Watching on the side during her main lesson—"a parents' day for grown-up pupils"—was Zoe's father Geoffrey, and during the class they got talking. He was not old, just a little older than Charlie probably. He had white hair, but black eyebrows. He was, thought Charlie, quite handsome in a rugged sort of way.

They got on well from the start, and as they watched Zoe go about her routines, he asked Charlie for her advice on his daughter. Despite her skill as a dancer, she was, he insisted, a normal young teenager who seemed to be going off the rails and had told him she wanted to give up dancing.

"The trouble is," he said seriously, "That her mother, my wife, is dead, and I feel that a woman to woman talk is in order. She really needs someone to pull her round, because although I may be prejudiced, she's a really good dancer."

Charlie smiled inwardly. They all said that. But watching Zoe showed that he was right. She was raw and still untrained to professional standards, of course—despite Felicity—but there was definitely something in the way she went about her dancing that seemed worth persevering with.

When the class was over and while the girls were changing into their street clothes, Geoffrey asked Charlie if she would talk to his daughter and persuade her to carry on dancing.

"If anyone can, I think you could," he said.

Before she could answer, Zoe came from the changing room and walked towards them, but before she reached them, Geoffrey quickly asked Charlie if they could meet to discuss things further.

"Would you like to come round to my house... or go for a drink if you'd prefer?" he suggested.

Charlie agreed it might be an idea in a couple of days.

They met, in fact, at Geoffrey's house. It was a typically suburban style two-up, two-down in a quiet cul-de-sac, and Charlie called there early one evening just as it was growing dark. Geoffrey, who was wearing a baggy old sweater with a pair of smartly creased sports trousers, ushered her in to the living room and switched on a tall standard lamp in one corner opposite a large, old-fashioned deep TV set. As he poured her a drink of red wine and invited her to sit in one of the two deep leather armchairs placed on either side of a bare fireplace, he told her that Zoe had gone out for the evening with some friends.

It was a very masculine room, and apart from the two armchairs there was a matching two-seat settee and a table light that was a miniature version of the standard lamp. A picture of an aeroplane— Charlie thought it might be a Second World War Battle of Britain

Hurricane fighter—hung over the mantlepiece, and there was an imitation coal gas fire in the grate. Very practical, thought Charlie.

There were various macho style ornaments littered around, and Charlie wondered how Zoe managed to live in a room like it, but guessed she had a very girly bedroom of her own. It also went through her mind that this had been the family home for a long time, but that Geoffrey had probably refurbished it when his wife had died.

Geoffrey—"Call me Geoff," he insisted from the start—was charming and full of Old World good manners. He did not sit until she did, and he was quick to stand and offer her a refill for her wine. He asked if she had eaten, if she wanted something, but Charlie refused.

"Well then, perhaps we can get down to business..." started Geoff.

For some reason Charlie felt that the ultra-serious way he said it was hilarious, and without thinking she started to laugh.

"Oh no..." said Geoff, embarrassed.

Charlie got control of herself. "I'm sorry," she said quickly. "I didn't mean to laugh. But yes, let's talk about Zoe."

Geoff seemed to recover as well and started to tell Charlie about Zoe's rebellious streak. "She never wants to do what I tell her," he finished lamely after outlining a catalogue of things she had not done for him.

Charlie remembered her own dealings with her father after her mother's death.

"It's quite natural," she said. "Most girls argue with their father. Quite vehemently sometimes. It's what little girls are made of. Not sugar and spice!"

Geoff nodded. "I think I told you," he went on, "Her mother died a few years back, and I've tried my best. But nothing I do seems to be right. She argues, nit-picks..."

"A real pain in the derriere," said Charlie.

Geoff nodded.

"I don't honestly think my talking to her would do much good. I don't think I'd be any better than you," Charlie continued. "But what might help is if I started giving her some personal one-on-one attention in class. At least, I can find out if she really wants to dance or if it's what she's telling you, that she's only doing it because you tell her to."

Geoff was grateful. "Oh, she wants to dance all right, deep down," he replied. "I've often heard her telling her friends that she wants to be a big star. But she's complaining because she doesn't seem to get anywhere, although I've told her over and over that she's still too young. I think it might help if you could do something."

They talked about Zoe some more, and Geoffrey repeatedly told his guest what a great dancer his daughter could become. Charlie listened, thinking that he sounded like her own father, but she did not say anything. Eventually, she agreed to give Zoe special attention in her classes, and the conversation drifted on to other, more general things about the village in which they lived.

Geoff, it turned out, had been an executive with a stockbroking firm, a bit of a high flyer until his wife had died, when, he admitted, he seemed to switch off in order to look after Zoe.

"I've always wanted the best for her," he said. "If only she'd listen to me a bit more."

In the weeks that followed, Charlie studied the girl carefully during her "special" sessions. She was fairly tall, but after her early lessons with Charlie now seemed to have stopped growing. Now she had quite a feminine figure, albeit with a slim, masculine waist and long, long legs. She had grown into a beautiful young lady, looking slightly older than her still young years, with long auburn hair tied back into a huge ponytail.

She often wore a black, figure-hugging, short-skirted leotard which showed off her figure in quite a sexy way when she moved. It was slinky, and often reminded Charlie of a black panther, and one day, for no reason at all, she told Charlie that her father had told her she must not wear it, even for lessons.

But Geoff was right, she obviously had a built-in talent. She could sing with a nice pleasant—what Charlie called "old-fashioned"—voice as well as dance. And she was a quick learner.

Zoe excited Charlie with her basic talent and potential, and under her careful supervision the girl soon outwardly regained the obvious love for dancing she had been hiding.

"I only told Dad I wanted to give up to get him off my case," she said one day. "He's always on at me."

It shouldn't have surprised Charlie, therefore, when a couple of weeks later she discovered that Geoff always collected Zoe after her lessons, waiting for her outside the hall where the classes were held. She was in her late teens now and was quite responsible, but Geoff was always there, and Charlie always made a point of speaking to him while the girl was saying her farewells to the other pupils. She told him how Zoe was progressing, and said she was happy with the way things were going.

One day, as they were speaking, Geoff seemed a bit vague, almost self-conscious. She gave him news of the lesson in her usual happy way—after all, she had been involved with dancing all afternoon—and then he suddenly stopped her.

"Look... I hope... well, I hope I'm not speaking out of line. But would you like to have dinner with me some time?"

Charlie smiled, surprised that he was so awkward and sheepish in her presence. "Of course, I'd love to."

"Can we say next Tuesday? I've—"

"That would be fine. Wher—"

He interrupted her. "I'll book a table. I know a new restaurant that's had some good reviews."

"OK, I'll leave it to you. I'll look forward to it."

Zoe was walking towards them.

"I'll call you to see where and when. See you on Tuesday."

"Yes, seven o'clock. I'll let you know."

Then he was gone, and Charlie stood there with a stupid grin on her face as Felicity came out of the school.

"You look like the cat that's got the cream," she said.

Charlie just grinned even wider.

That dinner was the first of several meetings in the weeks and months that followed. Geoff would take Charlie to restaurants and she, in turn, invited him to her house for meals. They got on extremely well at all times, and Charlie enjoyed the somewhat lively "debates" they had when she sometimes disagreed with his formal dogmatic statements about things. Geoff had strong views on almost every subject: the government, crime, driving, the bad manners of most people, particularly the young.

Surprisingly, Zoe seemed to ignore their meetings, neither expressing approval nor disapproval to either, and after about six weeks Charlie asked Geoff what Zoe did when they met.

"Goes out with boys or other undesirables, I suppose," snapped Geoff, and Charlie was quick to change the subject.

Every time they met, Geoff was a model of courtesy. He made a great play of always walking on the "outside" of Charlie, always opened doors—even car doors and making sure she was seated before he closed them—always stood when she did, and never once missed a "thank you", a "please" or an "excuse me". One day, he was waiting outside the hall in the rain wearing a trilby hat as protection, and when Charlie came over to him, he took it off as a courtesy. His hair was soon plastered down, wetted by the rain.

He was an exemplary gentleman, faultless, impeccable, flawless—sometimes almost irritatingly so because Charlie would have preferred him to relax more.

Although he seemed to prefer eating at restaurants—"posh caffs" was the way Charlie described them—they did occasionally eat at his house. On those days, they would sit formally at a dining room table, but when Charlie invited Geoff to her house the meal was taken informally with their plates on mats resting on their laps sitting around a low coffee table. Geoff always looked awkward at those times.

The one thing on which he was constant was his request for news on how Zoe was getting on with her classes. He had forthright views on dancing, as on most things, and Charlie was content to let him expound them as he wanted. She tried to be exact in her replies about his daughter, always veering towards the natural instinct to please a parent, but in general she was happy with the way things were going.

"I always knew she was good. Tell me how good," was the tone of his inevitable question whenever they met.

It was exactly the same yet again when she turned up for a meal at his house. He poured her a glass of wine and asked the question.

"Why don't you come along to see for yourself?" she suggested, "It's been a long time since you watched her."

Geoff agreed to attend the next week's class.

When he did turn up, Charlie saw Zoe was not wearing the slinky, sexy black leotard and was subconsciously putting a little more into her work. She was trying—too hard—but she was still good, and did a solo ballet sequence and a tap routine that was as good as could be. Charlie applauded her at the end of each, but noted that Geoff just watched with his head lowered slightly. Being too critical, she wondered.

After a break, Charlie suggested that Zoe show her father a routine she had been rehearsing, allowing her to sing as well as dance in order to show her father "what a good voice you have". Zoe grinned, went across to a sound system and changed a tape. She walked back to the centre of the room, watched by Charlie, Geoff and a couple of other pupils, and the music of the Rodgers and Hammerstein hit "Oh What a Beautiful Morning" struck up in a tinny piano sort of way.

Zoe swung into the song whole-heartedly, completed the lyrics, and went into a dance set, and was doing well until she started singing a second time. She had got to the line "the corn is as high as an elephant's eye" when Geoff suddenly called out.

"*An* elephant's eye. *An, an.*"

Zoe stopped suddenly, bemused, but as the music continued Charlie smiled.

"No, the girl is right," she said softly. "Everyone makes that mistake, but that's the way it was written, for a character. In any case, if it was 'an', you wouldn't be able to sing it properly. You couldn't help it coming out 'as high as a *ne*lephant's eye'." She felt rather like Danny as she said it!

Geoff was smouldering at the apparent snub, but he accepted it. The music stopped, and Charlie signalled to Zoe and the other girls to go and get changed.

"Sorry about that," she told Geoff, who was quietly feeling more than a bit miffed.

He shrugged, and when Zoe returned, he went off home with her without a word of goodbye.

Geoff turned up again with Zoe for her next class, and this time watched without saying a word. He and Charlie chatted amiably about Zoe after the lesson, and they carried on meeting up for meals fairly regularly. Quite a friendship grew between them, but was it more than just a friendship? Charlie soon started wondering whether or not she had fallen for Geoff, and he seemed to respond in the same way. He did not show outward emotion, but she had a feeling he too thought they were more than just friends.

But there were things about him she found "irksome". By now Geoff always attended Zoe's classes, and too often he interfered with what Charlie or Felicity told her. He would sometimes just watch, but more and more frequently he began putting in his point of view. If Zoe did just one thing wrong, he would call out—sometimes he was right, more often than not at odds with what Charlie was suggesting. Although Charlie always did her best to discourage him—in a friendly way—he was always there with an opinion.

"No, no. Do it like this..."

"Don't forget what I told you..."

Once, he even called out, "Just do it the professional way like I told you."

Charlie had to bite back the irritable words and thoughts that came instantly to mind.

Another time, Charlie was telling Zoe how, if she really wanted to be a dancer, she had to know many different ways of dancing.

She started to explain some of them, but Geoff walked over and interrupted.

"She can do anything like a real pro already," he said rather pompously. "Come on, Zoe, show her that new wing and a buck like I taught you."

Charlie tried not to laugh. "It's actually a buck and wing," she said. "Just a tap step with some extra sharp leg flicks. It's a sort of Irish clog dancing mixed with some high kicks and some shuffle and slide steps."

Zoe too tried not to laugh, and luckily Felicity came in at that moment and asked if anyone wanted a tea or coffee as it was breaktime.

There were other things as well. For instance, one day Charlie was again invited to Geoff's house for a meal while Zoe was out, and after he had offered her the usual drink, he turned the conversation to Zoe and suggested she was almost ready to become a professional dancer. She was good enough, she said. The TV was on, an old film, and Charlie couldn't help noticing that while they were chatting, Geoff talked, but kept glancing at the set to see how things were going.

On another occasion, he took her out for a meal, and when the waiter gave them the menus, he took them both, took a quick glance, then told her, "Hey, look, fixed menus. Two meals for the price of one. I think we'll have that one."

It was the first time he had done anything like that—normally allowing her a choice—and it was not quite what she expected from someone she suspected might be in love with her.

Charlie still had mixed feelings about her relationship with Geoff, although it took over a month before she felt she had to say something. Geoff had never mentioned their "relationship"—he had always been very formal about things—and for some reason Charlie felt indecisive about it all. One evening, she suddenly decided to tell him how she felt, but Geoff was in one of his stuffy moods, trying to be assertive, and wanting his own way about everything, including the conversation.

"It's just that... well, now that Zoe is doing so well, I just want you to know—" Charlie began.

"What? About the way you feel living your life through someone else?"

"No. No, not that. Although I must admit that watching other people dancing—and dancing well like Zoe—makes me feel somehow very inadequate."

Geoff pulled a face. "Inadequate? I don't see how. You've been at the top. You can't feel inadequate."

"Well, it's just that I love to dance. Used to love to dance," Charlie stammered. "It was my whole life, my real reason for being if you like."

Geoff did not answer.

"I just feel as if part of me is missing. Not dancing is like cutting off part of me."

Geoff's face was grim, a scowl forcing him to crease his forehead and pout his lips. "Have you ever thought of having therapy? Treatment?" he asked, rather crassly.

"A shrink?"

"No. Just someone to give you some advice."

"That makes me sound like some kind of a nut."

"Not at all. Just that you seem to have a bit of a mental kink…"

Charlie was starting to get angry, very angry. "You forget I've been ill, really ill…"

"That was a long time ago," said Geoff. "Get over it. You're as fit as me."

Really annoyed, Charlie stormed out of the house, got into her car, pulled on the driving gloves she still needed to wear because of the fuzzy feeling in her hands, and started the engine. Then just as suddenly, she switched it off, took her gloves off again, and stormed back. By now, Geoff was standing in the doorway watching her.

"How can you know how I feel?" asked Charlie in a voice that rose to quite a high pitch. "Have you ever had chemo?"

"No, but I'm sure if I did, I'd never let it affect me years after it was all over."

Charlie stormed away from him again, but Geoff made no effort to follow her and shut the door. This time though, Charlie sat in the car for a while crying, and it was some time before she started the engine and drove off.

When she got home, she pulled out her Gene Kelly video and fast-forwarded it to one of his dances. As the music built up, she tried to dance along with it. But it was uncomfortable—it hurt—and she fell, just catching herself on the front of the sofa or she would have been flat out on the floor. She was in floods of tears again.

The next morning her left ankle was really sore, and she wondered if she should go to the doctor about it. She decided against it, however, and the ankle stayed sore for just a couple of days before it then got better and she finally forgot about it.

But the whole incident did give her food for thought. Although it had been a high probability for a very long time, she now knew really deep down in her heart and mind that she would never be able to dance again.

That argument with Geoff was the first of a whole series of disagreements. Some big, some small. Charlie tried to keep away from arguments, but Geoff was obdurate in all things and then one day he once again started telling Charlie and Felicity what he wanted—and expected—for Zoe's future, reiterating how he thought they should help his daughter progress. Zoe, who was listening, tried to tell him to keep quiet, but he insisted on sounding off.

He was so unrelentingly adamant, however, that after listening for quite a few minutes Charlie felt she had to warn him off—something she did rather violently, telling him to let the girl develop at her own rate and through her own enthusiasm. She did not want Geoff to interfere in Zoe's future as her own father had done with her, and she made that quite clear as she spoke.

"Geoff, just let Zoe do her own thing. She's grown up. She knows what she wants, and she must do things in her own way, no matter what any of us thinks," she said.

"She'll do it my way or not at all," replied Geoff. "I'm her father. I know what's best for her."

"I'm sorry, but that's not always the case," insisted Charlie quietly.

Zoe had walked away, crying. Felicity stood by Charlie's side, but did not know what to do or say.

"You've done a good job so far, but the rest is up to Zoe. It's her life," Charlie went on. "You've got to let go. Once she's on stage, it's Zoe that has to do things, make her own decisions. Just let her get on with it."

Geoff was furious. "Zoe's... Zoe's... oh, what the hell." And he stormed off.

Charlie went across to Zoe and put her arm round the girl's shoulder. "He'll calm down," she said. "But it had to be said. I'm sorry."

"Don't worry about it. You're right," said Zoe. "He's always pushed me..."

"Just like my father did with me at the beginning," said Charlie with a reassuring smile. "That's how I know about it."

Zoe's tears finally calmed down and she went home—Geoff had already gone—and Charlie wondered whether or not she should have spoken. As she cooled though, she knew it had been the right thing, and she hoped Zoe wouldn't suffer as a result.

She also knew it was the end of her possible romance.

# Chapter 29

# LONELY AGAIN

During the few weeks Charlie spent trying to get over the "romance", she realised with a bit of a start that Geoff had never once actually told her of his feelings, nor had he even tried to kiss her. She told herself that she didn't really know anything about him, and with an inward smile she thought that she didn't even know if he wore false teeth or had artificial chest hair! How could she have ever thought she could be falling for him?

She realised too that she was all alone again. She had no family around her. No man, no one. No one except Aaron, Danny, Harry, Felicity, Zoe and a few of the dancers she knew from the old days. Dancing, she decided, was still her whole life, her entire reason for being alive, even though she could not take part in it.

Contrarily, despite that feeling, when Zoe unexpectedly left the dance school—Charlie heard she had signed up to an expensive studio in London—she herself decided to give up working at the dance school with Felicity. For a while, Zoe phoned her to tell her how she was getting on and said she had switched schools at the insistence of her father. She said she missed Charlie's "inspiring" tuition.

For her part, Charlie went back to her isolation and after-noons just driving round the countryside she loved so much. She adored the names of the villages she drove through: Norney, Golden Pot, Itchell—she wondered if there was a Mrs Mitchell of Itchell—and Tuesley, which she always believed she should visit on a Tuesday!

But slowly she became bored with them, and the drives eased off. As winter approached, she began to spend a lot of time on her own at home, simply sitting and looking through the large lead-crossed windows, taking in the bushes and trees in the garden. Most were almost bare, except one that had stumps of old branches sticking out on all sides like a ladder to its top, and there was one solitary pink rose still in blossom. A squirrel would hustle across the lawn, leaping the last few feet to safety. A couple of large blackbirds might peck their way across the still green grass. A neighbour's cat was always prowling like a junior grey and white tiger searching for prey.

Everything was always quiet, and the non-stop evolution of country life made her begin to think of her life itself.

She read somewhere that Dane had yet again either got engaged or broken off an engagement to his leading lady in a Broadway show, and it occurred to her that he always got engaged or broke off his engagement to his leading lady. And that made her think of the three big romances she'd had. Two with leading men in her shows. She had loved them all. She thought of her life as a dancer and singer. She had loved that as well. She thought of her favourite, friendly producer Aaron, and loved him for giving her a chance, and she thought of Danny and Harry and the songs they had written for her. She had loved them as well.

Then she thought and wondered about her life and future now, and she hated being alone. Even her friendly garden robin visitor seemed to have deserted her. She went into a state of depression, and barely left the house. She tried to think of all the lovely places she had passed on her lone drives over the months: the picturesque villages with strange names, none of them with shops except one that had a solitary emporium trading as a beauty therapy salon. There were the tall trees, glorious masses of greens in the summer, gaunt ramrods like rugby posts in winter, multi-coloured reds, browns and surviving greens in the golden autumnal light.

Now she could face them no more, and slowly she began to sink into a loneliness in her house. She stopped going to the Friday night gatherings at the club, took no more drives in the countryside near her home through the tree arches that lined the roads that she loved. No more seeing the young lambs, calves and foals in the fields, no more golden sunsets in the autumn. Instead, she drew the window curtains early every evening so she wouldn't have to look outside. No more television. No radio. She withdrew into herself completely.

With the eventual outbreak of spring, however, she began to get a yearning to be with people—with dancers. In an effort to snap out of her despondency, she rang Aaron and tried to talk to him as naturally and normally as she could about his shows, the latest films and other bits and pieces. It was forced.

Aaron was unusually quiet and let Charlie have full reign with her series of meaningless ramblings, but he knew there was obviously something wrong. Eventually, as she stammered to a finished silence, he asked her if she'd like to come to see him. They made arrangements, and a couple of days later Charlie went to London and met the producer in his office. He was all smiles, welcomed her like the friend she was, offered her tea and a comfortable seat, then asked if she was feeling any better.

"Well, yes. But I've been feeling… well, so miserable lately," she told him. "There's still this horrible tingling. Not quite numbness but a fuzziness in my fingers and hands and in my feet. It seems to be extending up into my ankles as well. For some reason, my feet often feel wet when they're not, and my fingers greasy."

Aaron let her talk.

"It sounds like I'm moaning, but I'm not really," she went on, her eyes getting damp. "It's still the after effects of the chemo, I think. It's better than the alternative, I suppose. But I can't dance anymore. It's too uncomfortable. It's always there and it's getting me down a bit."

Then suddenly all her feelings of despair and desolation came tumbling out. She didn't know why, but Charlie told Aaron exactly how her feelings had been going over the past few months—about the growing depression, everything, in detail.

"It's not just the physical feeling that I can't do anything," she said. "I just don't *want* to do anything. All I ever want to do is sit and mope. I know it's silly, but that's just the way I feel."

Aaron sipped his tea and looked sympathetic. His wife poked her head round the door of the office but when Aaron signalled to her, she realised something was going on and withdrew.

"I feel as if I'm limbo," Charlie continued, not noticing the intrusion. "I don't want to make it sound dramatic or theatrical and I know it's the oldest cliche in the book, but I feel like I'm locked up in a prison cell. I can't get out. I can't escape."

Then just as suddenly as she'd started, she stopped, and Aaron gave her a half smile. "You know, I'm glad you feel like that," he told her slowly.

"Glad...?"

"Yep, because I sensed there was something wrong when we spoke on the phone, and I want to make a proposition to you. and if you feel like that, I think it will help us both. Y'see, I need some help and the way I'm seeing it you're the girl who can give it to me. Danny and Harry are still busy writing, and they can't help. What I want is someone to give me professional advice on some auditions I'm holding for a new show."

Charlie was really quite staggered. When Aaron told her more about the show, her inner feelings told her she was intrigued and interested.

"The show's got some great tunes. Harry and Danny are just as brilliant as ever," Aaron told her. "I've already got a choreographer fella. He's already under contract, but he's a youngster from ballet and although he's got some good ideas, it's all starting to be a bit much for him. This is his first musical, and I know he won't mind some help from someone like you."

Charlie was instantly interested in helping, and when he had finished, she told Aaron she would love to become involved. He got out a tape and put some of the planned music for the show on a player to one side of the room. It was very good, and immediately Charlie got its feeling and wanted to show others how to move to it, although obviously she knew she couldn't demonstrate. But after her experiences with Felicity's local dance school, she also knew she had a natural aptitude that allowed her to explain the things and moves she wanted.

"It sounds like a great idea," she told the producer. "But are you sure? I don't want to tread on anyone's..." She stopped and laughed. "It would be more uncomfortable for me than them if I did step on their toes."

Aaron joined in the laugher.

"It's a great idea," he eventually told her. "I told Mark all about it and said you'd probably agree, and he's delighted."

"Mark?"

"Oh yes, Mark Valentine. He's the choreographer. I think you'll like him. He's got a lot of things about him that you had... have... and I think you'll get on well."

Charlie still had enough money from her time as a leading star not to have to work—put by in the bank and in savings accounts— but she agreed when Aaron offered her a small stipend.

"Not too much. I'm not made of money," he joked.

Charlie did not haggle about the deal, but having agreed to the job she felt it was a good thing that would allow her to do something positive to restart her life. Aaron gave her a date when auditions would begin, and Charlie left his office feeling much better than when she had arrived. Aaron's wife–secretary smiled at her as she went out and once she had got to the street, Charlie breathed deeply and a smile appeared on her face. She was happier than she'd been in a long, long while.

# Chapter 30

# BACK TO THE BOARDS

The auditions did not take long, and Charlie played a big part in helping choose the dancers, both the leads and the chorus. In no time, it seemed, preparations began for the show itself.

As always, Aaron rehearsed his shows in the actual theatre where they would be playing. Going there for her first day, Charlie got a train to Waterloo very early, allowing herself plenty of time to get to the theatre. When the train got in, she had almost an hour before her call.

She was determined to get the feel of the West End once more, and after queuing for a taxi, asked the driver to take it slow so she could look at the sights that had been so familiar to her. As he drove, Charlie had her window open so she could also hear the sounds of the city, and as they reached Trafalgar Square, she couldn't help noticing that there were still quite a few of the traditional pigeons still there—although they were supposedly "banned"—and a sudden flight lifted them off in a noisy swoop that reminded her of the many bird flocks at home, the rooks, the starlings and the others. But those thoughts of the countryside disappeared for a moment as she looked at Eros with excitement.

As the cab continued into Lower Regent Street, her thoughts returned to the flights of swifts, blackbirds, blue tits, robins and all the others that lived in her garden.

She still had plenty of time, so she asked the cabbie to drop her off where Lower Regent Street runs into Piccadilly Circus, and when she got out it was almost as though it was the first time she had seen the streets. She stood for quite a few minutes taking in the noise and the feel of masses of people: tourists, workers, people on holiday, old, young, middle-aged. She breathed it all in.

No one seemed to be speaking—many scurrying along looking at the ground and muttering anonymously into mobile phones—and Charlie got the feeling that she would have got as much communication from the trees around her home in the countryside. She was, she thought, a real country girl now, but being in the West End was exciting her, giving her a buzz. She began to feel part of things.

Although she knew it would be uncomfortable, Charlie had decided to walk the rest of the way to the theatre, about half a mile, but she didn't want to overdo it and walked across towards Shaftesbury Avenue quite slowly, concentrating on her old school girl habit of not stepping on the cracks between the paving stones because it took her mind off the aches in her feet. She tried to look passersby in the eye, but they invariably looked away, except for one young man with long hair who winked at her. Charlie smiled back. It was a happy day.

At the foot of Shaftesbury Avenue, she paused and looked up the curving street to see the row of theatres running along its length. The heart of show biz. She stopped, not only to look at them and delight, but to rest her aching feet. After a few minutes she continued along to "her" theatre and Aaron's show.

When she got there, slightly limping now and with her feet hurting, she turned down an alleyway at the side of the theatre to the stage door. Her first day back, and like a new girl on her first day Charlie went through the unattended door with a sense of awe, walked through the behind scenes area, and stepped onto the stage. There were others standing around in small groups, but Charlie just stared out at the front of house. There was the traditional "ghost light" off to one side, and another light high overhead, but without floodlights she could see the row upon row of empty seats, green backed and set in slightly curved rows for all the world like a robot congregation waiting to give a silent verdict on the performances they were about to see.

It was like a worldly wise old audience that had seen it all before, but there was a quiet over them all that seemed to Charlie just like a packed house of people waiting in silent anticipation.

She turned to look around her, feeling good, and saw Aaron and songwriter Harry chatting to someone she didn't know but who turned out to be director Max Bloom.

Almost immediately from one side she heard music played by a five-piece group that Max had called for, rather than just a rehearsal pianist, and as the first bars of the big hoped-hit song came out, she felt the old surge in her blood. Her muscles tensed, her legs twitched, her brain switched on and she wanted to dance. The music enveloped her inside and out.

Aaron looked up and saw her, and called her across to welcome her.

"Charlie, come on over here," he said, and she walked across.

Harry said his hello and left. Aaron introduced Max, then he called for an assistant to find Mark, the choreographer. Mark arrived after a few minutes—Charlie felt he had been waiting in the wings for the call—and when he arrived Aaron introduced him as well.

Charlie and Mark got along fine from the beginning, and after she had watched him conduct a short rehearsal of a routine dance, they all went for a drink at a pub opposite the theatre. That afternoon, Charlie just watched Mark putting some of the lesser dance members through their routines without saying a word, but she was impressed with the quiet efficiency he showed in dealing with "his gypsies" and felt an instant rapport. They were very much on the same wavelength.

Mark was in his early twenties, with a mop of dark hair that flopped over his brow, a muscular upper body and fast-moving legs and feet. He was a superb athlete in control of his body at all times, yet his social skills were a little less sophisticated. In a normal one-on-one conversation, he tended to stutter, sometimes even blush. It was an endearing trait, thought Charlie.

When he was in command of a situation, however, he was able to put over his points clearly and calmly. No hesitations, just an authoritative way of explaining things. Charlie found many of his ideas similar to her own, and in the coming weeks she only occasionally needed to suggest things that contradicted him. Otherwise, she simply backed him or made small adjustments and tried to show the dancers what they were both aiming for. It was a combination that worked well.

By now, although she still felt as if there was a thick rubber block under the arches of her feet and both her feet and ankles hurt when she walked or stood for too long, Charlie was able to figuratively grit her teeth and give simple walk-through demos of the dances, stepping slowly through the moves. But she still mainly used her hands expressively to show what was needed: palms facing up, palms facing down, sweeping them high and low and liltingly from side to side in a methodical, rhythmic, tidal way. She had discovered how to do this with Zoe, and the dancers for the show seemed to switch on to it well.

But this time around, being part of a show was different. Charlie realised how shallow most theatrical people were—playing a part all the time. Singers to a lesser degree than the actors, dancers to an even lesser degree than the singers. Charlie saw it and wondered how she had been part of it.

But even though she now knew more or less for certain that she would never dance again, she still loved the atmosphere, the aura, of show business, of the theatre. Yes, she still missed the quiet of the countryside. The open fields, the woods, the strange timelessness of a one-thousand-year-old church miles from the nearest houses—*what civilisation had there been there before?* she wondered—the beautiful thatched cottages and Elizabethan mansions, the friendly pubs, the animals and the birds singing. But back in town, there was a strange excitement that set the blood pounding in her veins. People rushing were no match for animals scurrying, the screech of cars and buses no equal to birds singing or animals calling, but it was exhilarating.

And now, she could look at the performers and be apart from them. Now they amused and irritated her in turn, so she concentrated only on her dealings with the dancers and choreographer, and to a lesser extent on the singers.

Surprisingly, in the first week of rehearsals for the new show, Charlie caught herself wrapping a scarf round her neck the way singers do to protect their vocal cords.

And slowly, she felt as if another romance could blossom with Mark. Life was good and she enjoyed it.

One day, she and lyricist Danny went for a late breakfast at a nearby transport cafe.

"Why do they always say 'good food served here'?" asked Danny, "They wouldn't tell you if it was bad food, would they?"

They chatted about all kinds of things, about the way the show was going, about funny incidents from their past musicals, incidental reminiscences about performers.

Charlie was feeling good, and she watched Danny chew on a piece of toast and marmalade for a moment.

"I thought you show biz types always had toast and caviar," she laughed.

"Oh no. Always marmalade," replied Danny. "It reminds me of the first line I ever wrote: 'Marmalade the table while Papa laid in bed'." He grinned. "That's the genius that got me started in this writing lark."

He finished his mouthful, wiped his lips, then suddenly became serious and told Charlie about Marguerite having an abortion. "And no, in case you heard the rumours, it wasn't mine. I don't like actors."

In an attempt to hide a sudden awkwardness, Charlie mumbled agreement and tried to explain how she now felt about show people. "I don't like actors either," she said. "I don't feel like them now. They're different."

Danny nodded. "I reckon you've felt like that for a long time," he told her. "D'you remember when I came to see you down at your house, amongst the Coco Pop fields? I asked if you'd come back and work on a show with Harry and me. You turned me down. I had a feeling about you being disenchanted then, and on reflection, it would have been a bad time for you to come back, probably with us especially. But now you're working for Aaron. Well, he's surprisingly sympathetic. He's the best thing for you..."

"Aaron is a friend."

"Yep, a good one. He's a real rogue, but he helped Harry and me get started—and you—and he's done a tremendous job for us all. It's all down to him. Yep, a good guy."

They lapsed into silence, but after a while, Danny spoke softly again. "That time I did ask you to come back," he asked, "Did you ever think of starting up again, just as a singer? You had a pretty good voice."

"I probably still have," she laughed, then turning serious, she added, "It wouldn't have been the same. Singing was OK as an add-on, but all I want—wanted was to dance. That was it for me. Dancing, the only thing. It was my life. I couldn't have gone on a stage without it."

Soon after that breakfast, Max called a two-week break for the dancing and singing rehearsals, wanting a couple of new songs and needing to put the emphasis on the straight acting part of the show. Charlie stayed at home and pottered in her garden enjoying the countryside, but with her mind staging dance routine after routine.

Her first day back in the theatre after the break started with a bit of an eye opener. A pleasant surprise. As Charlie walked through the stage door and onto the bare stage, a rehearsal pianist was playing a sweet, melodic tune. By his side were Danny and Harry the writers.

"It's called 'Blue Is My Colour'," they told her.

"Oh, it's my colour too. My favourite," she told them.

Danny gave her a knowing wink. "That's what we thought," he said. "We wrote it for you, but it'll fit the show perfectly."

The song—dedicated as it was to her—pleased Charlie, and she worked out a quick routine to slot in with it in the show. When Mark arrived, she told him about her idea, and he agreed it was just what was needed to lift a part of the show that had seemed to need a boost.

It was a good song, and although the dance routine for it was endearingly flowing, it did require a modicum of agility. Trying a tricky turn while rehearsing it, the girl playing the second lead fell awkwardly and hurt her ankle. She could not stand, and as Charlie watched with a strange feeling of having been there before, Max arranged a lift to take her to hospital for a scan.

When he came back more than an hour later, the assistant director who had taken her said the girl had ligament trouble and had been sent home in an ambulance with her foot tightly strapped. It would take weeks, possibly months, to get better. She was out of the show. Aaron immediately called for auditions to find a replacement.

Charlie, who had never ever had to audition for a stage show—only for her film role to see how she photographed—recommended both her former dance school partner Felicity and her star pupil Zoe, and phoned them to invite them to audition for the part. Both were excited at the thought.

For a few moments after making the calls, Charlie wondered if she was just suggesting the two of them for sentimental, friendly reasons—because she knew Felicity had always wanted to be a dancer and that Zoe was dreaming of becoming a star—then her professionalism took over and she knew they were both good enough. And in any case, she reasoned, it would not be her decision whether or not either got the role.

They come in separately. Zoe tried to look adult, but with her hair tied in a braid at the back and curled round to finish just to the side of a central parting on top of her head in a kind of "rose", she only succeeded in looking younger than she really was.

Despite that, she and Felicity danced well at their trials, and both were asked to perform a second time. Mark, Max and Aaron all agreed they both deserved to be cast, and both were given parts in the show: Felicity in the part they had auditioned for—she was certainly good enough—and Zoe in a smaller but significant role because of her lack of experience. Everyone was delighted at Charlie for putting their names forward.

Charlie herself enjoyed it all. And then Mark asked her if she'd like to join him for dinner after one rehearsal.

# Chapter 31

# MARK

That dinner was the first of several over the next few weeks, and on their rare days off—Sundays mainly—Charlie and Mark would spend the whole day together. They went for picnics when it was hot, for drives out into the countryside where Charlie pointed out the delights and sights of her "home" life to her new boyfriend, and for leisurely lunches at the seaside.

It was, to Charlie, all that a boy-meets-girl story should be, and if there was no music readily available, she would often sing something suitable to Mark. He was a good listener, and when no one was watching, he would often dance round her as she sang. He no longer blushed when they were together.

As for the show, when rehearsals got under way it was decided that Felicity should give up her role in her own school and a new teacher was bought in to run it in her absence. Charlie helped make the decision on the replacement, a young girl called Belinda Hazel in her early twenties straight from a dance academy.

For a short while, Charlie spent a few hours each week supervising Belinda and the school, noting with pleased interest the changes she started to bring in, but for the rest of the time she continued in London with the show rehearsals. Eventually, she rented a flat fairly near the theatre in London.

The show was starting to take its final shape, with Charlie and Mark still working well together getting the dancers sorted out and seeing each other on a regular basis. Mark made Charlie laugh, and it seemed they were both talking the same kind of "gypsy" language. Soon, Charlie felt herself falling for him, and it seemed that he began to feel the same way.

"It's funny, but it seems to me that leading ladies in shows always fall for their leading man," she told him one evening. "But it's not quite the same with us, is it? I mean, well, I'm not a leading lady and you're not quite the leading man."

She got tongue-tied, and Mark smiled at her.

"I thought I was your leading man," he replied.

"You know what I mean," she added slowly, "We're both kind of important to each other, aren't we?"

They both laughed, and Mark bent forwards to kiss her. "If I was a leading man and you were my leading lady, it'd be obvious that I would fall for you though," he said when they broke.

It was easy for Charlie to enjoy Mark's company, and when, after rehearsals had finished early one evening, he put on a tape of the show's music and asked her to dance with him, she tried. He held her ballroom fashion and they smooched rather than danced for a while, but then Mark automatically tried to spin her as he would have done in a full show number. Charlie felt a cold stab at the side of her foot and pulled away.

"I'm sorry, it hurts," was all she could say.

Mark was solicitous and anxiously helped her to a chair.

"I'm sorry. I got carried away..." he said.

They agreed there would be no more dancing, but Charlie somehow felt that something had gone from their blossoming partnership.

On the work front, however, they continued to spark with each other, bouncing ideas back and forth and working things out in the same way as before. It was just that when they met away from the theatre Charlie now sometimes felt slightly ill at ease.

Opening night soon loomed. Pre-opening try-out runs were held, and Charlie was involved with Mark, Max, Aaron, Danny and Harry in making the little adjustments and refinements they all felt were necessary. Charlie was once again amazed at the flexibility of the dancers in switching from a well-rehearsed routine to one of the alterations without making a fuss.

Then the show opened, and they all waited for the reviews anxiously. They need not have bothered. The pre-opening bookings had been very healthy. Now, even before the critics poured their high-sounding and wordy praise on the show, it had somehow got around that the show was more than just good, and the box office reported a huge boost in sales. The show was fast becoming another success for Aaron and his writing team of Danny and Harry.

Charlie and Mark carried on seeing each other, but he began to take less and less interest in the show and seemed to be quite busy in other ways. He reckoned his part was done, and he started looking for a new show as Charlie kept a protective eye on the dancers.

Mark's new project came when he got the offer of a job in Dubai and decided to take it.

"It's just too good for me to refuse," he told Charlie. "It'll do my career no end of good, and the money's just fabulous."

"How long will you be away?"

"I don't honestly know," said Mark. "They're going to pay me on a week to week basis, and it's so good I've got to make it last as long as I can. Anyway, the backers tell me they have plans to move in to London and New York, so I want to keep in with them."

Once again, Charlie felt the same dull feeling of rejection she'd had before, but she did not say anything.

# Chapter 32

# DANCE AGAIN, BALLERINA

She stayed on in her rented London flat until Mark flew off about a month or so later, then feeling sorry for herself she returned home to the country. By now, she had bought the dance school from Felicity and had decided to go back to teaching, running it herself with Belinda, the teacher who had been bought in when Felicity started rehearsing for the show.

One afternoon, Zoe, her former protégé from the school, called on her unexpectedly and watched her take one of the classes. Afterwards, they went back to Charlie's house for tea. Charlie felt that with her new life she might like something stronger, but was pleased that Zoe had not yet taken up the "sophisticated" and customary glass of Prosecco.

Zoe told Charlie that her father had been quite irritated when she had been called in for the show audition and had won a part in it by herself, but she said he had now come round and seemed pleased that she was getting on.

Charlie had momentary thoughts about Geoff, but they soon passed and he didn't really seem to matter to her anymore. The talk moved on and Charlie poured tea for them both. She realised as she did it that the cups did not match. Something that would have worried her at one time.

"I don't know how you can come back and stagnate down here again," said Zoe as she sipped at her drink. "It's so exciting in London…" She spoke with the wide-eyed thrill of discovery that a youngster would normally show in her circumstance.

Charlie nodded. "I've probably grown out of the need to be excited," she replied.

"But they say that when you fall out of love with London, you fall out of love with life."

"Something like that," agreed Charlie. "So maybe I have got a little disenchanted with life."

"I don't believe that for a moment. And I don't see how you can just put the show and all that behind you and come back here to a dull old life."

Charlie smiled at the younger girl. "Oh, I don't know that it's really so dull," she replied. "I'm still involved, and that's the important thing. It doesn't have to be with floodlights and all glitzy and glamorous. I just love being involved with dancing."

Zoe left it at that, and in the weeks that followed, Charlie allowed her life to move along slowly, with routine lessons. Some boring, some showing just a brief spark from one or other of the pupils, one or two with youngsters who showed real talent. But always, as she had said, it was dancing, and she was involved. She convinced herself she was enjoying the quiet life once more.

Although she was now completely concerned with running the school, Charlie made a point of buying a ticket and going back to London for the day to see the show again—to be reassured that both Felicity and Zoe were managing all right. She watched them and the other dancers perform their gyrations, their rhythmic swirling and twirling, their graceful movements to accompany the lilting music, and she loved it all.

Halfway through the second act, she began wondering. Was Zoe right? Should she stay in a backwater and vegetate? The show excited her. She could see the bits and pieces she had created being re-enacted, and she enjoyed it all.

But she wasn't certain that she should get involved again, so when it was over, she made a conscious effort not to go backstage, and instead went home quietly without anyone knowing she had been in the audience.

Then it was back to the school and, with her visit to London in mind, Charlie decided to put on her own show with the pupils there. She knew it could not be anywhere near the same in either quality, size or effort, but she wanted to be involved again somehow. With Belinda's help, she worked out a programme, and the show went ahead.

Not wanting to be thought "precious", Charlie simply billed the show as the school's annual concert. It was, she told everyone, mainly for parents and relatives to eulogise over their children. Under her expert tutelage, it began to develop, and although many of the young dancers were really too young to be performers in such an event, the show began to take good shape.

The concert was in the form of a series of linked themes, with the pupils of varying ages putting on their own small part of the overall display. It was, if you like, a professional amateur show.

There was a small local theatre near her home—about a hundred and fifty seats—and Charlie took it over for the day of the show, and tickets sold quickly. Rehearsals moved on faster than she expected, and Charlie was caught in the fever as the children grew excited— over-excited in the case of many of the younger girls.

Soon it was opening night. Curtain up at 6 p.m.

The first act was uneventful, although Charlie was a bit apprehensive as midway through she watched critically from the wings before nodding approval as a line of little dancers, some as young as three, paraded round the stage in a twisting crocodile before going off to loud parental applause, whistles and hoots.

Into the second act, and things were again going well as the show moved on towards its close. As a finale, one of her other young girls—a pretty six-year-old with blonde hair—took over the stage for a solo performance. She had come to the school months before to "do dancing", and at first had leapt around like all the other very young girls. But she had a natural talent that came to the fore easily and very quickly. Charlie had encouraged her to express herself from the start.

Now she was on stage, wearing a miniature tutu and with a headband that blended in with her hair but revealed two highly coloured roses on either side just covering her ears: one red and one white. Charlie recalled her own performance in a similar show at the same age.

Light-coloured sequins on her bodice reflected the floodlights from way behind the audience, and more lights from the wings picked out the silver spangles on her small tutu.

The song was from one of Charlie's old shows—she could clearly remember working out the routines in her early days on a West End stage—and the girl performed her spins, twirls and jumps in a mature, well-trained way. It was not exactly as she had been trained, but the girl added some extras that helped the dance match the music perfectly. Despite her age, it not only looked good, it was technically good as well and was far better than the grubby old stage deserved.

Although she was only young, it was all there, a whirling, enchanting performance that from the start won the audience's combined hearts and was shown by the ovation at the end. The girl faced left, right, centre, and bobbed down, curtseying and smiling.

In her mind's eye, Charlie remembered her own shows as a child. Through her mind flashed all the hard work and dedication she had needed throughout her career, giving up virtually everything else so she could dance. She had loved it; it was a necessity for life. Now it had to be channelled in a different direction.

Her mind came back to the present time. As with her own childhood, when the girl's dance ended, some people in the middle of the audience stood to applaud. Although day dreaming about her own early days of dance, Charlie showed her real professional show biz appreciation and quickly signalled for the next piece of music to start up quickly. As with her own show as a child, it was a lively piece in contrast to the sweet tenderness of the main dance and was meant to cover the girl's exit from the stage. The girl heard it and started dancing enthusiastically from side to side and across the stage.

She got caught up in the music again and began a small shimmy, then—still wearing her pink ballet pointe shoes—swept effortlessly into a rigorous soundless tap. The audience whooped and whistled, thinking it was still part of the show.

Charlie heard the girl's father on the other side of the stage calling for her to come off, "this instant", and had another flash of memory of herself as a child. As she had done so many years ago, the girl took no notice.

"If you don't come off *now*, I'm coming on and dragging you off," said the father in a loud uncompromising voice.

Charlie turned to look at him. "Leave her, for a moment," she called.

Reluctantly, and with the audience still applauding, the dancer took a giant balletic leap into the wings.

"How unprofessional," said her father, his voice again unbending. "You've been to plenty of these shows. You should know how to make an exit by now."

The girl smiled back. She was still dancing in her mind, celebrating her birthday. This was the day she became six.

On stage, the curtain came down on the end of the show as the parents and friends applauded as if it were a giant hit in the West End or on Broadway. The young dancer hopped to the wings and smiled at her father and at Charlie, who hurried across the closed stage to hug her. Like the girl, she was still dancing in her mind, celebrating the success.

For Charlie though, that dance had been a recreation of her own dancing as a six-year-old. Her life had been recreated; her life had pirouetted full circle.

She knew then that the only important thing in her life was not necessarily playing to an audience, but to dance. And to be involved in dancing despite her dodgy knee.